"You're a good man, Jaxton Stone." Naomi sniffled.

No, he wasn't. He was having all kinds of inappropriate thoughts about her. Wondered what she would do if he bent and brushed her lips with his own. But he couldn't. Damn it all, he just couldn't.

"Sometimes," he said, "doing what's right for everyone takes a huge leap of faith, but I promise you, it will all work out all right in the end."

She turned to face him and he warned himself not to move. Not to stare at her lips. Not to lean in close to her. It was the hardest thing in the world to let her go.

"You're a good mom," he heard himself say, forcing himself to relax. "Have faith. Trust your heart. It'll never lead you astray."

She peered up at him, blue eyes wide, her hair spilling around her shoulders, and he felt himself falling…falling…

"Good night."

He ran.

Winning the Rancher's Heart

PAMELA BRITTON

First Published in Great Britain 2017
By Mills & Boon, an imprint of HarperCollins*Publishers*
1 London Bridge Street, London, SE1 9GF

Large Print edition 2017

© 2017 Pamela Britton

ISBN: 978-0-263-07193-1

Our policy is to use papers that are natural, renewable and recyclable products and made from wood grown in sustainable forests. The logging and manufacturing processes conform to the legal environmental regulations of the country of origin.

Printed and bound in Great Britain
by CPI Antony Rowe, Chippenham, Wiltshire

With more than a million books in print, **Pamela Britton** likes to call herself the best-known author nobody's ever heard of. Of course, that changed thanks to a certain licensing agreement with that little racing organization known as NASCAR.

But before the glitz and glamour of NASCAR, Pamela wrote books that were frequently voted the best of the best by the *Detroit Free Press*, Barnes & Noble (two years in a row) and *RT Book Reviews*. She's won numerous awards, including a National Readers' Choice Award and a nomination for the Romance Writers of America Golden Heart® Award.

When not writing books, Pamela is a reporter for a local newspaper. She's also a columnist for the *American Quarter Horse Journal*.

Dedicated to my darling Lysy Loo,
the daughter of my heart.
We love you, Alysa Panks.

Chapter One

"Is this it?" T.J. asked, his left elbow brushing her own as her son wiggled on the old Ford's front bench seat.

Naomi Jones stared at the sign hanging above the dirt road, clenching her palms against the sweat that formed.

Dark Horse Ranch.

"Yes." She sighed. "This is it."

"It doesn't look like much of a ranch," said her other child from her shotgun position. Samantha sounded about as enthusiastic as a dental patient about to undergo a root canal, but these days her teenage daughter didn't sound enthusiastic about anything.

She had a point, though, Naomi admitted, but she knew from experience you couldn't see much of the place from the road. Just a bunch of valley oaks dotting the acreage and the needle-straight line of a road, one that headed toward some low-lying foothills not too far in the distance. It was dusk and the sun had just started to set behind the hills. The dew point had risen and it released the scent of herbs in the air.

New life, new beginnings, she reminded herself.

Goodness knows she'd made a mess of the old one. Not at first. At first it had been heaven on earth. But then Trevor had died and everything had changed, and not for the better. These days Samantha was either a perfect princess or perfectly horrible. It was clear she needed to rein her in. And T.J. Poor T.J. had been bullied since his first day of elementary school. She hoped like heck the move would help.

Here we go.

Her old truck rattled forward. Someone had hit her pickup in the back and taken off without leaving a note. She didn't have the money to fix it, so duct tape held parts of the bumper together. She should probably have it fixed before it flew off on the freeway or something, but that was what this move to California was all about, too. A good-paying job. A place to live—for free. And, once she sold her home in Georgia, money in the bank.

"Wow," T.J. said.

She'd been so deep in thought she hardly noticed their surroundings. She looked up at her son's gasp of amazement and spotted it. Beyond the oak trees, nestled into a craggy hillside, stood a house. A very big house.

"I know, right?" she said, guiding the old truck toward the redwood-and-glass monstrosity. It should look out of place in the middle of the country and yet the home seemed to have sprouted from the very rocks it sat upon. She'd watched enough shows about architecture on television to know it'd been designed by a naturalist, someone who wanted it to look indigenous to the landscape, and had probably cost a small fortune.

"Is that where we're going to live?" T.J. asked with a tone of reverence.

She glanced at Samantha to gauge her reaction, but as usual, her thirteen-year-old had her head buried in her phone. Then again, in her present frame of mind, they could probably pull up to Buckingham Palace and Sam would pretend indifference.

"We're actually living around the left side. In the maid's quarters."

Sam snorted. Her daughter hated her new job title: housekeeper. One of many things Sam had given her grief about when she'd learned they were moving.

"Can we go inside?" T.J. asked. He pushed his thick-framed glasses up on his nose.

"Not the big house," Naomi said, smiling when she spotted the way his red hair stuck up on one side. They'd had the window down at one point. "We need to settle Janus into his new digs."

She glanced in the rearview mirror. The Belgian Malinois must be lying down because Naomi couldn't see his head between the bars of the plastic crate.

"He's going to love it here," T.J. said, wiggling on his seat.

At least one of them was happy with the move, although they weren't completely free of Georgia just yet. She still needed to go back and arrange for all their furniture and belongings to be stored and/or sold. And she'd have to move some of it out west, which meant another long drive.

"I thought you said there would be horses," Sam grumbled as they pulled up in front of their new home.

"They're here." *Somewhere.* According to the owner's sister, Lauren Danners, they'd built the horse facility out back. Lauren had been the one to hire her because her brother, Jaxton Stone, was always out of town. Hooves for Heroes was a therapy center for soldiers with PTSD, although she'd never seen it. A state-of-the-art facility. New, she'd been told. Very expensive.

She pulled up to housekeeper's entrance on the left side of the main house. Slipping out of the truck, she tucked her cell phone in her back pocket and took a deep breath of the chamomile-scented air. It had rained recently; that was the reason for the moisture in the air. She could smell the earth and the wild oats that grew between the trees. The moisture had settled on the granite stones that ringed the base of the house, turning them a dark rose color. A door had been placed in the middle of the wall—an ornate maple door with a fan-shaped paned window set into the top of it. Narrow windows sat on either side of that door, a small deck with redwood steps leading to the entrance. She wanted to buy some plants for the railings when she had some extra money.

"It doesn't look like much," Sam said.

"Wait until you see the inside."

Lauren had shown her around the fully furnished apartment when she'd flown out for the interview. Three bedrooms. A kitchen. Even a family room that overlooked a back patio with a pool right outside. Not her own pool, of course, but the owner's. She'd been told her kids could use it, though, as long as she checked with Mr. Stone first.

"Why don't you let Janus out?" she asked T.J. "He can check out our new place, too."

Her son dashed to the back of the truck, dodging suitcases and boxes to get to the beige-colored kennel. Poor dog had been cooped up for at least three hours.

"Use the leash," she warned. The last thing she needed was her husband's ex-military dog running off and getting lost. That would be a disaster.

"Can't we, you know, find a place of our own to live?" Her daughter's face was a mask of distaste as she stared around her. "I don't want to share a house with someone I don't know."

Naomi resisted the urge to make her own face. "We're not sharing a house, kiddo. We have one right here." And it's free. And furnished. And requires no commute.

Sam flicked her long brown hair over a shoulder. "Yeah. The servants' quarters."

Was it illegal to spank kids in California? She doubted anyone would blame her if she did. "Sam, please. Give this a try."

"Whatever." She flounced off, heading for the front door.

T.J. came up beside her, Janus by his side, the dog's dark eyes catching on something near the front of the house, although what she couldn't tell. He was forever looking for trouble, compliments of his military training.

"Don't worry, Mom. She'll get over it."

The fact that her ten-year-old son tried to console her shouldn't surprise her. He'd been doing that for the past two years, ever since Trevor had died.

"I hope so, bud," she murmured.

She'd been told the front door would be open, and it was. The apartment, which took up a whole corner of the owner's mansion, was just as spacious as she remembered.

"Wow," T.J. said again.

Definitely bigger than their place in Georgia, not that Sam would admit it. She just slumped down on the couch to their right, eyes glued to her phone.

"I'm going to go meet my new boss." Naomi tried to inject perky self-confidence into her voice. "Sam, can you and T.J. try to unload some of our stuff?"

Sam didn't answer, just kept clicking buttons.

"Sam."

Her daughter eyed her from above the top of her phone. "Fine."

She winced inwardly. The whole journey out to California, she'd tried to convince her daughter that the move was for the best. They'd be near the kids' grandparents once they made the move out west, too. They'd be living on a ranch. They could even have their own horses down the road once she sold the house. Sam had always loved horses. But Sam hated to leave her friends. She didn't like California, although she'd never been there before. She hated that her mom would be a housekeeper. Why couldn't she do something different? Why couldn't they stay in Georgia? And on and on it'd gone.

"I'll be right back," she said, trying to hide her disappointment. At least T.J. was happy. Her son was going from room to room, sounds of "wow" and "cool" being emitted periodically.

As if she didn't have enough to worry about, a sullen teenager only added to the mix. Jaxton Stone's sister had said he was a nice man: the perfect brother, she'd said. He worked super hard, which was why he needed a live-in housekeeper. Apparently, her new boss was always off somewhere in the world. He ran a military contracting company. She'd had to Google what that was, a sort of army-for-hire type of thing. They provided protection for corporate executives, too, something she'd never heard of before, but was apparently necessary if the company was big enough that it could afford to pay a ransom. She'd been shocked to read just how dangerous foreign travel could be for the head of a big company, and her new boss made a living keeping those corporate head honchos safe. A very good living, by the looks of it.

Off you go.

She stepped outside and skirted the house to the main entrance. At least her surroundings were pretty spectacular. The home sat on property that looked like something out of an old Western movie, or maybe *Bonanza*. Rolling hills were covered by dried grass, trees casting inkblot shadows on the ground, taller mountains in the distance. She'd had to cross through those mountains to get to Via Del Caballo, so she knew the ocean lay on the other side. It might have rained this morning, but it was clear now, a few patchy clouds off in the distance. She took a deep breath of the freshly scented air and then squared her shoulders. Lauren had constantly mentioned how great her brother was. She hoped her boss's sister hadn't fudged the truth.

The front door sat atop a row of steps like the opening to a Mayan temple. She was just about to make the sacrificial ascent when a sound caught her attention. A dog sat on the massive porch that framed the front of the house. It stared at her curiously from its position by a redwood chair with maroon cushions.

"Hey there, boy," she said, climbing the stairs quickly. Some kind over overlarge terrier, she thought, smiling at the way tendrils of hair came together at the crown of its head and made it look like it had a Mohawk.

"Bad hair day?" she asked.

The dog just thumped its tail. Skinny little thing. She wondered if it were ill or something.

She smiled down at it and eyed the place. Should she just walk in? Ring a bell?

She pressed the doorbell, stepped back, the dog watching her as she stood there, then moved forward and rang the bell again.

Was he home?

She'd been assured someone would be there to greet her this morning. And the apartment had been unlocked. Maybe he'd stepped out?

She wondered what to do. Wide beams stood above her, the wooden rails reminiscent of pictures she'd seen of Camp David. It smelled new. Like varnish and wood and fresh paint.

He must not have heard me. She peeked through one of the massive windows that lined the front. She didn't see anybody, so she went back to the door, turning the handle just to see if it was open, not to go inside or anything.

The alarm nearly deafened her. She had to cover her ears it was so loud. The dog that'd been on the porch ran away so fast she wished she could do the same.

Whoo-a-whoo-a-whoo.

What had she done? She hadn't even opened the dang thing.

Dear Lord.

She stepped back from the door, staring at

it, as if she could somehow will the alarm to shut off.

It swung open.

Blue eyes stared down at her. That's all she caught a glimpse of before he went back inside. Through the open door she watched as he turned toward an electronic console on the wall, pressed some buttons and silenced the alarm.

Her ears rang. Her face blazed. Her smile nearly slipped from her face.

"Good morning." She tried to brazen it out.

He slowly placed his hands on his hips, and as Naomi looked into his gorgeous eyes, she knew nothing would ever be the same again.

"Do you always just walk into people's homes?"

The redhead's smile grew even more strained, and he recognized the grin for what it was—a show of bravado that fooled no one.

"I didn't walk in, I promise." She lifted her hands. "I just tried the door."

"Soooo you could walk in?"

"No, no." She shook her head, a mass of red hair falling over her shoulders. "I was just seeing if someone was here. I wasn't going to walk in."

"Mom!" Behind her, a dark-haired girl came to a stop on his gravel driveway. "Are you okay?"

She turned to greet the teen. "I'm okay." She waved her away. "Just a little misunderstanding."

A little boy, younger than the girl and with hair as red as his mom's, skidded to a stop next. "Man, that was *loud*."

"I take it those are the kids?" he asked.

She glanced back at him. "Yup."

Which confirmed that she was Naomi Jones, although her Southern accent gave it away. The friend of a friend that his sister had interviewed and loved, and whom he'd been forced to hire because Lauren felt sorry for the single mom of two. That wasn't surprising given that his sister had been raising a child all on her own, but that would soon change since she'd met Brennan Connelly.

"Can I see the inside of your house?" the boy asked, lifting up on his toes as if he might be able to peer over his mom's shoulder.

The girl smacked him on the head.

"Ow!" the boy cried.

"Come on." The teen gave them what could only be called a glare of derision. "Let's let Mom do her *housekeeping* thing."

His gaze caught on the woman in front of him, just in time to see her wince. "I'm so sorry."

He'd have to have been a real jerk not to accept her apology. His men might call him a hard-ass, but it really wasn't true. Well, most of the time.

"It's okay." He stepped back from the door. "Come on in."

"Thanks."

She glanced around, her gaze coming to rest on a granite water sculpture at the center of the main foyer. The sound of running water soothed troubled souls, his included.

"I love your house." She stopped in the middle of the foyer, her eyes—the prettiest shade of blue he'd seen in a long, long time—traveling around the interior. "It reminds me of a guest lodge or something."

"Thanks."

Those eyes landed back on him. "I'm Naomi Jones, by the way."

He could tell she wasn't sure if she should hold out a hand or simply stand there and keep smiling.

He took the guesswork away from her and stuffed his hands in his pockets. "Nice to meet you."

He saw something flit across her eyes, something that told him he might have just offended her, or maybe disappointed her. "You, too." She stuffed her own hands in her pockets.

Interesting. Usually mimicking someone's gestures was a sign of submission, but he doubted that was the case here. He'd seen her tip her chin up a tad. Those bright blue eyes of hers had grown a little less friendly, too.

"So, those were your kids?"

"Yes. T.J. and Samantha."

"And you've settled into the apartment?"

"Well, no. We only just got here. I was told to come straight to you when we arrived. So you could meet me."

Check her out, his sister had said, although he hated the way saying the words made him feel. His sister had said she was perfect for the job, but that didn't mean he would think so, too. He'd agreed to hire her as a favor. He'd been telling himself for the past two weeks that he should trust his sister's judgment, but as Naomi stood in front of him he wondered what the hell he'd gotten himself into.

"Why don't we go talk in my office?" He motioned that she should follow him past the sunken living room that overlooked the front of the property and up some stairs to his left. He'd had very few people to his private retreat. He could probably count the number on one hand, but he wasn't surprised by her reaction to the vaulted ceilings and the wrought-iron balustrade as she followed him up the wooden steps. It'd taken a year to build the place, and another three months to build the massive covered arena and apartments out back. He'd spent those last several months flying back and forth between his corporate offices in San Francisco, interviewing hippotherapists and psychotherapists, and securing the purchase of the livestock for his ranch. It'd been a hell of an endeavor, but he'd gotten it done.

"My sister tells me you've done this before?"

"Well, not quite," she said, taking a seat opposite his desk. He watched as she immediately shifted first left and then right, solidifying his own thoughts about his new furniture. Not comfortable. He'd hired a decorator, and he'd begun to suspect that she valued form over function. He liked things the opposite way, something he'd clearly neglected to convey. In his line of work, things needed to be efficient. Someone's life might depend on it.

"I used to work as an event planner, and before that, I worked for a hotel doing the same thing. But I started out in housekeeping. Worked my way up while I attended college, that sort of thing."

He'd known that. He'd read her résumé a time or two. "Why do you want to move all the way out to California?"

She stared into her lap for a moment, resting her hands on her jean-clad legs, sunlight from the tall windows in front of her emphasizing the red of her hair. "The kids' grandparents are moving out here." She looked up and met his gaze. "My kids love them. I didn't want Sam and T.J. to be that far away."

"So you chucked it all?"

He didn't mean to sound critical, but he could tell by the way she furrowed her brow that she took it that way. "We don't have anybody else. No other family, no aunts or uncles, and life in Georgia is...challenging."

"More challenging than moving all the way to California?"

There went that chin again. "We needed a change."

A big change. At least from the sound of things.

He leaned back. He sat opposite her since he didn't need to see the view. "This job won't just be about housekeeping. I know that's what my sister told you, but it's going to be way more than that."

She tipped her head, leaned forward a bit. Her body language told him she didn't mind this change of plans.

"You'll still be keeping house to some degree," he explained, "and managing my household—buying groceries and whatnot—but whoever works here needs to be flexible, too. They need to understand that one day they might be asked to cook for me when I'm in town, or clean a guest apartment, or help one of our guests in some way. It won't be easy, but it'll be interesting. You do know how to cook, don't you?"

"You wouldn't ask me that if you'd tasted my Southern pecan pie." She beamed, and he had to admit she didn't look a thing like he'd expected. He'd expected older. More...harried-looking. She had two kids and he knew that couldn't be easy.

Drop-dead gorgeous, that's what she was.

Even in an off-white long-sleeved T-shirt as plain as day. He didn't normally notice such things, not when all he cared about was if someone could do a job properly, but the visual image in his head was so far from the reality that it startled him.

"What about you?" he said. "Do you have any questions?"

"Yes." She pinned him down with a stare like an entomologist would a cricket. "You won't be bothered by two kids and a dog, will you?" She looked around her as if envisioning two terrors inside his home.

"I would expect them to stay out of the way."

And suddenly she appeared amused, her blue eyes lighting up from within, her whole face transforming, and if he'd thought her beautiful before, that was nothing like the way she looked with a smile on her face.

"I can't keep my kids in a kennel."

"No, of course not, but kids are always off doing things, at least in my experience. As far as your dog, I would appreciate you keeping him on a leash, at least until we know how he'll react around horses."

"You don't think *your* dog will mind having a new dog on the property."

"What dog?"

Her brows drew together. "The one on your porch. Or it *was*. It ran off when the alarm sounded."

"What?"

"By the front door. But like I said, it ran off."

"I don't have a dog."

"No?"

He shook his head. "If you see it, please let me know. I'll have to call someone to catch it."

"No. Don't do that. It's better to try to re-home a stray."

"We don't know it's a stray."

She frowned. "I think it is. It looked skinny."

And she cared. With concern clouding her eyes, she looked younger. She couldn't be much older than thirty.

Younger than you.

Much younger.

"Let me know if you catch it and we'll go from there."

She nodded. "Anything else?"

"One last question."

She waited quietly. He admired the way the sunlight set strands of her hair afire before he admitted he shouldn't be noticing that type of thing.

"What if you change your mind?"

"About what?"

"The move. Working as a housekeeper. Living on the ranch."

She lifted her chin a tiny fraction, but enough for him to realize she was sensitive about the issue. "I won't. We even drove my old Ford truck all the way out here. And I've started the school enrollment process for my kids. They'll be all set to start at their new school in the fall."

He studied the woman in front of him. Lauren

had told him Naomi worried that her husband's death had affected her kids far more deeply than she'd surmised. That they were having problems in school and that a move all the way across country would be good for them. He couldn't say he agreed. Then again, he didn't have kids, so who was he to judge?

"All right then. I guess we'll see what happens."

"Terrific."

"And your first task will be helping to organize a party I'm having here in a couple of weeks. Local military brass. Short notice, but I'm sure I can easily pull strings and get people here. You'll have an unlimited budget to make it an affair people will remember. I want to make a big splash."

Her mouth dropped open. "I—"

"You've planned events before, or so you said."

He saw her take a deep breath. "Of course I have. I just didn't think I'd be starting so soon."

"Is that a problem?"

"No. Not at all."

"Good, then I'll take you on a tour of the ranch next."

She seemed surprised again.

"Unless you'd like to settle in first."

"No, no. That's okay."

"Good." He glanced at his watch. "And before I forget, here's some information I put together for you. My cell phone. Email. Etcetera." He slid a manila envelope forward. "Meet me in front of your apartment in ten minutes."

She lifted a hand, saluted. He lifted a brow. She smiled and stood up, envelope held in front of her like a shield.

"It was nice to finally meet you."

"Same," he said with a dip of his head.

He watched her slip away, but when she left he spun his chair so that it faced the windows. Maybe he shouldn't have left the hiring of a housekeeper to his sister. He had a feeling

Naomi Jones might prove to be a handful, although he had no idea why he felt that way.

Her eyes sparkled.

As if she saw the world from the big end of a telescope and what she spotted amused her. Usually, he hired people who were far more serious, but he supposed that was to be expected given the nature of his work. Naomi seemed… complicated.

He hated complications.

Chapter Two

"Can I tour the ranch with you?"

T.J.'s face was imploring and it killed Naomi to shake her head. "Honey, there'll be time to show you around later today. Let me spend some time with my new boss first."

"But I thought you weren't going to start work until next week," he said.

She'd thought so, too, but she should have known her new boss was a workaholic. His sister had told her how often he was out of town. That he was driven and impatient and yet the kindest man she'd ever get to know. She'd have to take his sister's word for it. So far she felt... nervous. He had the ability to escalate her pulse, and not because he was good-looking, although he was that, with his dark hair and blue eyes. Handsome and intimidating as hell.

"Plans changed." She brushed her hand through T.J.'s hair. "But I promise to explore with you later on today."

When she got off work she would make sure to show T.J. the ranch, although she'd forgotten to ask Jax Stone about her hours. And what days she'd have off. And a whole host of other questions because when she'd looked into his eyes she'd just sort of gone *ooohh*.

Someone beeped a horn. Janus stood up from his position at Sam's feet and began to growl.

"Nein," she softly told him. That was all she needed to say for the dog to rest his head again. That was the last thing she needed—for Janus to start attacking the door. "Stay inside," she

told her kids, although she doubted Sam heard her. Earphones didn't quash the sound of music that emanated from the tiny white buds. Her daughter would be deaf by the time she was fourteen.

"Can I go see the pool?" T.J. asked, eyes filled with hope.

"No."

His lower lip stuck out. "But Mom…"

"Just stay here. Sam." He daughter continued to tap something out on her phone. "Sam!"

That got her attention, but she seemed completely put out that she had to remove one of the buds from her ear. She did everything but roll her eyes.

"Keep an eye on T.J."

T.J. wiggled. "I don't need a babysitter."

The horn beeped again. Janus barked. Naomi turned to the room and said, "Stay."

"Mom. I'm not a dog."

"I know that. I meant all of you. Don't leave."

She slipped outside before T.J. could start complaining again. "Sorry," she told her new boss, drawing up short at the sight of the all-terrain vehicle he'd arrived in. It looked like something the military would use—all camo paint and big black bumpers and a cab framed by a roll cage.

"Was that your dog I heard?"

She nodded, her face coloring a bit because it was only then that she realized she hadn't told his sister exactly what kind of dog she'd be bringing with her.

"That did not sound like a small animal."

Once again she found herself tipping her chin. "He's a Belgian Malinois."

He knew what that was, she could tell by the way his blue eyes narrowed. "You have a Malinois?"

She nodded, decided that she should just spit the rest of it out. "He's an ex-military war dog."

His lips pressed together before he said, "What are you doing with an MWD?"

"He was my husband's."

Trevor.

Her high school sweetheart. The man she'd known instantly that she would marry, even as young as she was. She tried not to let her emotions show, but she saw Jax's gaze hone in on her own. It still hurt, although she'd hoped, goodness how she'd hoped, that it would have faded by now. At least a little bit. She prayed the move would help. Less of a reminder of what her life had been like before.

"You took possession of him after he died?"

She nodded. "Smartest thing I've ever done."

He stared at her a long time. "Come on," he said. "I'm sure you want to spend time unpacking when we're done here."

"It's fine," she said, forcing a smile as she slipped into the passenger seat. "How far away are the horses?"

"Not far," he said. "I wanted the guest quarters to be within walking distance of my home."

Jaxton Stone was rich. Not that she hadn't already known that. Not that she cared, but she could tell he was more than just well-off.

She'd found out about Dark Horse Ranch through Trevor's best friend, Ethan, who'd taken on the role of surrogate brother over the past year. Ethan's brother-in-law Colt had told her Jaxton owned the company Colt's brother, Chance, used to work for, and that they'd been in combat together once upon a time. And that Jaxton was the type of man who'd give his left kidney to someone. It was Ethan, Colt and Chance who'd convinced the reclusive Jaxton Stone to move to Via Del Caballo and build his therapeutic horse ranch for combat veterans. Naomi loved the idea so much she'd asked if he was hiring, and voilà, here she was. Except given their description of the man, and then after meeting his sister, she'd expected some-

one completely different. Guarded. Not this…
stern taskmaster who didn't seem to have the
muscles to smile.

"I love your home."

He put the vehicle in gear, the clutch lurching
them forward so that she grabbed the roll cage
to steady herself, the metal cold beneath her
fingers. It was far cooler than she'd expected.
She'd be chilled within a matter of minutes in
her long-sleeved T-shirt and jeans.

"Thank you," he said, shooting her a glance,
looking like any rancher on any given day, on
any other average ranch, in his black cowboy
hat and jeans. The road followed the curve of
the hillside, and she gasped at what stood on
the other side. A massive equestrian complex,
one made out of thick beams and with a steeped
roof and tall windows across the front. It was
all off in the distance, but close enough that she
and the kids could walk, and all tucked away
in a little valley behind his house.

"Wow."

She hadn't meant to say the word aloud, but it escaped before she could stop it.

"It turned out nicely, I think."

He *thought*? The ranch was a showplace. Long, rectangular buildings were usually plain and ugly, but whoever had designed his house had also designed his barn. It had thick beams jutting out, not just across the front, but along the sides. Massive double doors—two stories high—were set into the front so they could be opened or closed, but they were cleverly designed so that it looked like the short end was all one big wall of windows. It wasn't just a barn, she realized then. It was an arena.

Amazing.

It wasn't that she hadn't seen stables before. Ethan's sister-in-law, Natalie, owned an equestrian facility twice the size. It was the sheer newness of it all that blew her mind, that and the knowledge that before his arrival, none of it had been in the center of the valley, one with a small lake in the distance and hills that had been browned by the June sun.

He drove forward again. "I'd like to have the party down here, in the arena, so people can mill around and see what we've built. I'll invite some of the country's leading experts on post-traumatic stress disorder. Anyone who needs a room can stay in the guest quarters."

And he wanted to do this how soon? She gulped at the thought, but something told her Jaxton Stone didn't know the meaning of the word *failure*.

"We'll need to ensure we have plenty of food on hand, and maybe hire a caterer if you think it'll be too much. You should probably get me a list of local media. I'm hoping they'll take one look at Dark Horse Ranch and spread the word about what we hope to accomplish here. I want this facility to be the best therapeutic ranch on the West Coast. I want to change lives here. Help people. Make things better."

She turned to look at him, stunned to realize this wasn't just a passing fancy or some kind of tax write-off. She could hear the sincerity in his voice, earnestness mixed with hope and maybe even longing.

He cared.

"Let me show you the arena and the corrals and the horses we've purchased for the program first. That's something Colt and Ethan are helping me out with. I don't know a whole heck of a lot about horses, but I'm learning."

For the first time he had become animated, showing her the state-of-the-art, climate-controlled arena—actually driving through the center so she could see the iron stall fronts to her right and the polished wooden beams—every inch the masterpiece that his home was. The kids would go nuts when they saw it.

"The horses have been carefully selected for

the program." He motioned toward a dark bay horse that peered at them curiously from the other side of a stall front. "And they're turned out to graze in the evening, something that's good for them."

He showed her the turn-out pens next, driving behind the barn.

"The pastures are so green compared to the hills."

"We're on an aquifer. That's where the water for my lake comes from. That's what keeps everything green. Natural springs." He pointed toward the horse pens. "The Reynolds family could have charged me a small fortune for this property, but they sold it to me cheap. Actually, their home's just a few miles away from here as the crow flies. They still ride their horses out by the lake."

She smiled at the mention of the Reynolds family. She adored Colt and Chance and their sister, Claire. Particularly Claire, who'd taken such good care of Janus when he'd been in her care. Claire owned a military dog rescue and she was married to Ethan, who was a veterinarian.

"This is my favorite animal." He pulled to a stop in front of one of the horse corrals, getting out and heading toward the brown horse that walked toward them. "His name is Zipping Down the Road. Zippy for short. He used to be some kind of famous show horse, an actual world champion or something, but his owners retired him a few years back and he's been a therapy horse ever since."

She watched from her seat in the ATV as he walked up to the animal in question, holding out a hand, letting the horse sniff it before moving up next to his head and patting his neck.

"Looking for a treat?" he softly asked. "You know I have them somewhere, don't you?"

Who was this man? she found herself wondering, watching as he fished a baby carrot out of his back pocket and then gently fed it to the horse. His whole face had changed. Gone was the stern taskmaster. In his place stood a man with soft hands and warm eyes.

"Come here and pet him."

Okay, so there was the taskmaster again, but that was okay. She smiled because she'd been worried the kids would hate him. That her new boss seemed cold and distant and that he wouldn't like her children. But for the first time she saw the man who'd spent millions of dollars on a state-of-the-art facility for wounded warriors. A nice man. A caring man. A man with a gentle spirit.

Their gazes connected as she slowly moved up next to the horse.

"He's gorgeous," she said, and she couldn't hide her smile because it felt so good to pet one again. It'd been years, but she'd always been a horse-crazy girl. "I bet you were really something in your younger years," she told the animal, leaning in next to his nose and inhaling the sweet animal scent that only horse lovers understood. The horse did the same thing right back, smelling her loose hair and tickling her ear and making her giggle.

When she drew back she felt his gaze on her, her smile fading at the look on his face.

"What?" she asked.

He stepped away. "Nothing."

For some reason she felt the need to explain her reaction. "It's been awhile since I've gotten to pet a horse."

"So you've been around them before?"

"Oh my goodness, yes." She patted the animal on the softest part of its body, its muzzle, a place that felt like velvet. "When I was younger I used to ride all the time. My mom showed horses and I did, too, up until her death when I was sixteen. My dad died at the same time. Car accident."

And even after all these years, it still ached

like the dickens. She wasn't all that close to her in-laws. They hadn't approved of her being a blue blood. That's what Trevor had called her. He must have seen the twinge of pain in her eyes because he crossed his arms and drew himself up, the softness in him fading.

"We should get back." Had her words upset him? "You have a lot of work to do," he added.

He'd gone back to the uptight, aloof business owner, and for the life of her she didn't know why. She was the one with a sad past. First her parents and then her husband had died. Some days, it just didn't seem fair.

"Sure."

She reluctantly returned to the vehicle, gazing at the sorrel horse that watched them drive away. They headed back in silence, and Naomi wondered if she should ask him about her kids, if it'd be okay to show them around, but something made her hold back.

"Thank you for the opportunity to work with you," she said when he dropped her off.

"Don't thank me, thank my sister." He glanced at her quickly. "I'll expect you to start work at eight tomorrow morning. Feel free to show your kids around. You might not have time over the next few weeks."

He left her standing there, the tires even kicking up a little bit of gravel as he headed back to the garage on the far side of the house. Naomi watched him drive away with dread in her heart.

What have I done? she wondered.

And was it too late to change her mind?

Chapter Three

She would be here any moment now. He listened for her footfalls on the steps leading to the second floor. She had her own entrance to the house, through the kitchen, and he suspected she'd make use of it today.

He'd given her the pass code and instructions for his alarm yesterday, although he probably should have given her some kind of schedule, too. An oversight he would soon rectify. He stared out the row of windows that stretched across the second story of his home office, not really focusing on the view.

She still wore her ring.

And yesterday, when they'd talked about her husband's dog, she'd seemed lost. It had hit him hard for some reason. Maybe because she reminded him of his sister, who'd been through the same thing. There was just something…sad about her that had touched him when she'd told him about the Malinois, and then later, when she'd been petting Zippy.

His gaze slid over the front of his property, watching for movement in the brush. *Old habits die hard.*

Something stared up at him. Jax froze.

A dog. Big dark eyes held his gaze. If not for the contrast of the dark hair against the muted gray trunk of an oak tree, he wouldn't have seen him at all.

"Well, I'll be—"

She really *had* seen a dog. There'd been a part

of him that had wondered if she'd imagined it. Maybe confused a fawn for a canine. Or a coyote for a domestic dog.

"Am I late?"

He didn't turn around. "That dog is back." It was crazy the way the animal stared up at him, almost as if he saw him through the glass. Maybe he did.

"Is he brown?"

He nodded.

"Mohawk?"

"What?"

"Never mind." She came forward. "Where?"

He pointed. "Out by that tree."

The smell of her body lotion or perfume or whatever wafted toward him. Vanilla and lemons.

"We should try to catch him."

She sounded as Southern as Georgia peach pie. He finally looked away from the dog to peer over at her. Even in profile she was deeply and extraordinarily beautiful. She'd worn her hair loose around her shoulders, the bulk of it resting against an off-white sweater. An ambient morning glow filtered in through his windows and highlighted the paleness of her skin and the gorgeous blue of her eyes.

"Stay here."

He didn't give her time to respond; frankly, he was almost glad to leave her side. He didn't like noticing how stunning she was. She worked for him. Her looks were something he didn't want to dwell too deeply upon, so he stepped away from her, ducking through the entrance of his office and turning left, toward the massive stairwell that bisected the house. He'd always thought stained wood and wrought iron balustrade just a tad over the top, but it served its purpose well. He headed straight for the front door.

"Do you have a leash?"

She had clearly ignored his order to stay put. Why didn't that surprise him? "No."

"Maybe I should go get one of mine."

He burst out onto his porch. The dog didn't move. He headed toward the tree that it cowered behind, noting the matted fur and the skin that hung off its bones like a coat that was too big. It seemed to be some kind of terrier breed, an overgrown Toto that'd gotten too big for the basket. And it looked like it had a Mohawk. That was what she'd meant earlier.

"That's him. That's the one I was telling you about."

"Go call animal control."

"No."

He glanced over at her sharply. She didn't seem to notice, just moved past him. "Let's see if we can catch him first." Her feet crunched on the rocks of his gravel driveway.

"Leave it alone. It might have rabies."

She stopped, turned to face him, the look on her face the same one she no doubt gave to her kids when they said something ridiculous, like maybe a candy bar would be good for breakfast. It raised his hackles. He'd been up for hours and he was pretty sure the scruff on his chin and the ends of his hair stood up on end, and he was tired, which might explain his cranky mood.

"I sincerely doubt it has rabies. Like I said, we need to catch it." She turned back to the animal. "Poor thing. It's been weeks since he's had a good meal."

"All the more reason to call animal control."

He turned to go back to the house to do exactly that, but she half turned and caught him with a "No," and it was hard to say who was more startled, because she stared down at their joined hands for a moment, then jerked her gaze up at the same time she released his fingers.

"I mean, please don't do that. Not right now. Let's see if we can catch him first."

"I don't think he wants to be caught."

"Come here, Fido," she crooned softly, once again ignoring him.

"Fido?" he heard himself say.

"Shush," she told him.

Shush?

She hunched over a little, and God help him, his eyes dropped to her backside and the way her jeans clung to her curves and he forgot his disgruntlement and cursed inwardly instead.

"There you go," she crooned softly as she moved toward the oak tree near the edge of his driveway. "Don't be shy. Remember? We met yesterday."

The dog didn't move and Jax found himself eating his words because the mutt didn't run away at all. He reached out with his nose, sniffing her.

"Do you have a rope?"

"Uh, I have no idea." And if he did have one, who knew where it was. He'd paid someone to move him in. The past couple months had been a constant game of hide-and-seek.

"A belt then?" She glanced up at him, still

standing next to the dog, gently stroking his head, her wedding ring catching his eye. "Or a tie?"

"I'll go see what I can find."

This wasn't how he'd envisioned his morning going at all. He'd imagined her sitting across the desk from him. Had planned to give her a to-do list a mile long. That would have kept her out of his hair. Instead he found himself standing in front of her and contemplating the odds of her obeying an order from him to let animal control deal with the situation.

"You know what? You stay here. I'll go inside. I have a leash we can use." A smile stretched across her already wide mouth.

"Here. You take him," she added.

But the moment she moved, the dog bolted. "Hey," she cried, making a lunge for him. She landed on air, her breath rushing out of her with an *oomph*.

She immediately rolled onto her back, Jax

torn between revulsion and dismay because she'd managed to cover the front of her pretty off-white sweater with streaks of dirt.

"That little jerk," she said, using her hands to sit up. The dog ran away like he'd been struck by a bolt of lightning. "Now we'll never catch him."

"Told you we should have called animal control."

"I can't believe he did that."

He moved forward, holding a hand out to help her up. She took it willingly, and the way she smiled at him, her eyes bright and twinkling, her whole face lit up, it socked him in the solar plexus. Man. She could sell rain to Noah with that grin.

"Perhaps you'll listen to me next time."

He hadn't meant the words to come out sounding so stern, but he saw her smile falter.

"Perhaps I will."

She flicked her chin up and Jax couldn't decide what her best feature was, her stunning eyes or the power of her grin.

She pulled her hand out of his grip and brushed herself off. "Looks like I'm going to have to change." Her hands dropped back to her sides. "Maybe I can get my kids to catch him when he comes back."

"Maybe."

What the hell was wrong with him that he watched her hands on her breasts, that a part of his mind went on its own little safari wondering if they were as firm as they...

"Meet back in my office when you've changed."

He turned away before she could spot the bright shade of red that ran up the side of his neck, at least judging by the heat that scorched his skin. And the way he clenched his hands. Or the way his whole body had tensed.

Mother of two, remember. Widow. Still wears the wedding ring.

Did he need a better reason to steer clear?

"WHAT A MESS."

Naomi stared at her reflection in the mirror and spotted a leaf in her hair. Could she have made a bigger fool of herself?

"Are you sure he ran toward the road?" T.J. asked.

He was excited beyond belief at the prospect of a hunting expedition. He'd even changed into a camouflage outfit.

"I'm sure. But you're to stay within sight of the house, you hear me?" He ran out of her bedroom. "And take Sam with you."

"Really, Mom?" her daughter drawled.

"Really, Sam," she called back. She didn't know what had happened to her sweet daughter, but she'd disappeared into a cloud of puberty.

She dashed into the bathroom as big as a hotel room to fix her hair, the sound of the front door closing behind her kids echoing through the house. She couldn't believe the size of her new digs. It was nearly a hike from the front door to the back to her massive bedroom and the walk-in closet that housed her pathetic wardrobe.

It took her a quick second to brush her hair. She stepped back to examine her long-sleeved white shirt—her standard uniform for life, that and jeans. It might be June in California, but the lack of humidity made it feel like winter in Georgia.

Off you go for round two.

Her own entrance to his home was at the very back of her apartment, beyond a door that might look like a linen closet but wasn't. There was a hallway with a washer and dryer to her right, and beyond that another door that led to his house. The security buttons beeped as she punched numbers. A long beep sounded when she'd finished, followed by a *snick* as the door unlocked. She half expected him to be on the other side. Maybe pop out from around the hall-way that led to his kitchen.

And what a kitchen it was—like something

that belonged to a reality cooking show, one where celebrity chefs and top models cooked. Large rectangular terra-cotta bricks made up the floor. The entrance at the end of her hallway was an arch, one made entirely of bricks. As were the walls. In the far wall sat a giant stainless steel hood with a double stove beneath.

She reached out a hand and glided a finger across the island in the middle. The off-white marble was cold to the touch. Not even the fixture that hung above it—three lights made into one—could warm its surface. The whole house felt that way, she thought, entering the main foyer. It was stunning. A true work of art, but unlived in, which was strange because she knew Jax's sister had lived in the apartment she'd taken over, and she must have cooked in the kitchen a time or two. She paused for a moment at the entrance to the living room, trying to put her finger on what it was.

No plants. Not even a fake one.

To her right sat a sweeping staircase, and just beyond that, a cobblestoned fireplace. But if she owned this gorgeous place she'd have stuffed a massive ficus in the corner. Maybe even some pointed palms at the corners of the couch in the sunken living room. Something that would catch the light from the double row of windows and set off the granite floor. Whatever. Not her place, and it never would be. What *was* her problem was the granite floor. She could see her reflection in it and she didn't want to think about how much work it would be to maintain it. No wonder he needed a housekeeper.

She turned toward the stairs, but she paused as she stared out the cathedral windows along the front. T.J. ran through the grove of trees across the road, clearly on the trail of something. Sam followed reluctantly behind, her brown hair long and down her back, head bowed.

She had her phone.

Dear Lord in heaven. She might have to have

the thing surgically removed. For a moment she contemplated telling her to put the thing away and keep an eye on her brother, but the property was fully fenced. How much trouble could they get into searching for a dog? Besides, she needed to get to work.

Work.

She had a list of chores he wanted done daily. And now he wanted help planning an event. She placed her hand on the smooth burl railing. And he wanted her to act as a maid. And a hostess. Lord, it sounded like she'd be busy in the coming weeks. But busy was good. Busy kept her mind off thinking of Trev and how much she missed him still.

"Knock, knock," she said, rounding the corner of his office. There was a double row of windows downstairs and the same in his office, although she could see the A-line of the roof from where she stood because the second-floor windows were snug up against it. Jax sat behind a massive desk made out of a slab of burl that matched the stairwell railing.

"Take a seat." He waved toward the same chair she'd sat in yesterday.

"Okay, I meant to ask you, but what is it made out of?"

He motioned with his hand as if the answer should be clear. "It's a tree root."

She felt her brows lift. "Of course. What else would it be?"

He seemed puzzled by her lame attempt at humor. It made her wonder yet again what she'd gotten herself into.

"Are your kids looking for the dog?"

"Out there right now." She took a seat, the wooden surface uneven and uncomfortable.

He leaned back in his chair and he seemed such a contradiction. He lived on a ranch, yet he looked more like the CEO of a big corporation with his short-cropped hair, the ends dipped in gray. He wore a white button-down shirt, and from what she could tell, jeans and boots. No cowboy hat today. Probably no big buckle. No wide smile of greeting, either. His sister was so sweet and open, yet his face was as closed as the garage door on the other side of his home, his entire demeanor unapproachable. Even his office was a contradiction. It was meant for show. All wide-open space, expensive furniture and sparse furnishings, and yet he had a Lego cowboy sitting in between two massive computer screens, one of them with a COWBOY TOUGH sticker stuck to the back.

She caught him staring at her. Something in his eyes made her smile fade.

"So I thought it would be a good idea to give you a to-do list this morning." He glanced at the screen on his right.

She shifted in her seat. A to-do list? In addition to her housekeeping list? The man knew how to keep a woman busy.

"Great."

He slid a sheet of paper in her direction. "You'll see the first item on the list is to call animal control."

She almost shoved the thing back at him. "No." And she even surprised herself with the sharpness of her tone.

"Excuse me?"

It was the third time that day she'd said no to him, but she didn't care. "I told you we should catch him."

"He's a stray."

"He's lost and alone and scared. I see it in his eyes. I refuse to send him to a place where he'll feel even more alone and afraid."

He shook his head. "You presume he's lost. It's more likely that he was dumped."

Her stomach lurched at the thought. Who would do such a thing? "I still don't want him to go to a shelter. They'll kill him."

"Not necessarily. Someone might adopt him."

"A dog like that? One that doesn't want human company? No."

She could tell he wasn't pleased by her argument. Great. Five minutes into her meeting with the man and already she'd managed to antagonize him.

"Just let the kids try to catch him. I'm sure once Tramp realizes we want to help him, he'll come around."

"Tramp?"

She nodded. "From the movie. Doesn't he look just like him?"

"I don't know. Never seen it."

She sat back in her seat, winced when her spine made contact with the back. "Never?"

He shrugged. "What can I say? I don't watch a lot of TV."

The poor, sad little man. "Well, trust me. He looks just like him."

"I'll have to take your word for it."

She glanced down at the list he handed her

again. "Research caterers?" She tipped her head up. "I don't have a computer."

Another blank stare. "Not even a tablet?"

She shook her head. "I had one, a laptop I mean, but my daughter dropped it on the way here. It fell out of the back seat of my truck and shattered the screen. I have a smart phone, but that's it."

His look was akin to someone being told ten plus ten was two. For some reason, it made her want to smile. Nerves, she told herself. Smiles and silly giggles had always been her go-to reaction when she was tense.

"Will that be a problem?" she asked.

He slowly shook his head. "I'll have a laptop delivered to you by the end of the day."

Of course he would. She glanced down at the list again. "I guess that means I can't do items three, four and five, either. I'd need access to email for that."

"You don't have email?"

"Of course I do, I just think it'd be easier to research and solicit bids from caterers using a laptop instead of a phone, don't you?"

He pressed his lips together. "Okay then. Maybe now would be a good time to go over the housekeeping list I gave you yesterday."

"Sure."

His brows drew together. "Is there something wrong with your chair?"

She realized then that she'd been shifting around in it a lot. "This thing is like some kind of medieval torture device. Clearly, whoever you asked to decorate this place didn't actually expect anyone to live here."

He kept doing that—kept looking at her like she had Christmas lights hanging from her nose. Just then the phone on his desk rang. He glanced at the number and answered. He listened intently for a moment and then replied in perfect French, something she didn't understand, and he spoke it so fluently and so well that it was her turn to have her mouth drop open.

Who *was* this man?

She'd been expecting a sun-bronzed, boot-wearing cowboy. Maybe someone quite a bit older than her. But someone who was kind and approachable, like his sister. Instead she sat across from Clint Eastwood in his younger years. Maybe when he'd played the role of Dirty Harry.

He hung up and said, "All right, let's go over the list I gave you yesterday."

"I don't have it with me."

"That's okay." He clearly had a copy because he read from it. "Floors. As noted, use your best judgment when those need to be done. I'm not around a lot of the time, so you might not need to do them very frequently." He met her gaze for a moment, but quickly looked away. "Windows, as needed. You'll find all the cleaning supplies in a pantry in the kitchen. I've tried to think of everything you'll need. Let me know if you'll need anything else."

She nodded, not that he was looking at her.

"Dusting, empty the trash, cleaning the light fixtures—that's all self-explanatory, and like the floors, I'll leave that up to you."

He set the paper down. "One thing I wanted to mention was laundry. It's not on the list, but I was going to ask if you'd mind doing mine in addition to your own."

"No. I don't mind at all." Could he see how flushed her face had turned at the thought of folding his underwear? She hoped not.

"I don't expect you to iron. And if something needs to be dry-cleaned, I'll take care of that myself." He picked up the list again. "Let me know if you think anything needs to be professionally cleaned. Carpets. Drapery. And keep your eye on fixtures and whatnot. This is a new home, but things can still break."

"Got it."

He set the list down again. "Did my sister tell you what I do for a living?"

She sat up straighter. "Yes."

"Good. You should know I have accounts all over the world, which means I travel a lot."

"She mentioned that, too."

"Although I've slowed down lately. I've made a commitment to my sister and nephew. I try to spend as much time as I can with them, although sometimes it's just not possible—my work takes me away from home. That's where you come in. I'll need you to keep an eye on the place. I've hired someone to manage the ranch and all its livestock affairs, but he's coming all the way from Texas and he won't be here for a couple of weeks. Until then, the Reynoldses are a big help."

"That's who we should call about Tramp. Claire Reynolds has her dog rescue." She couldn't believe she hadn't thought of that before. "She'll know what to do."

He nodded. "Good idea. You can add that to your to-do list."

The phone on his desk rang again. She expected him to pick it up. Maybe start speaking in Russian or something. Nothing would surprise her with this man. Instead he ignored the call.

"Back to the security of the ranch." He leaned toward her. "No houseguests."

She lifted her brows. "None?"

"Not unless they're authorized by me."

"Not even the tooth fairy?" She couldn't resist. He just seemed so stern.

He'd gone back to staring at her again. "Tooth fairies are the exception."

"What about Santa?"

"Approved."

"And the Easter Bunny?"

"Roger that."

"My kids will be relieved."

Lord love a duck, was there an actual living,

breathing smile on his face? She'd made him smile. She had no idea why that filled her with such a sense of accomplishment, but it did.

But then the smile faded. He stared at her. She stared back, and she realized she liked him. She had no idea why. He hadn't exactly been all warm and fuzzy. She'd spent most of their time together arguing with him and he didn't seem to mind. Actually, he seemed to enjoy their tooth fairy conversation.

"Anyone else?" he asked, lifting a brow.

"I'll let you know."

"Good." He glanced at his open laptop again. "Once you receive your laptop you'll receive a pass code for my wireless network. Under no circumstances is it to be shared."

"Not even with my kids?"

"They can have it, too. Just not anyone outside the ranch."

"Got it."

"You should also be aware that there are security cameras. They're discreet, but they cover a wide variety of angles, so be mindful."

"Good to know in case one of my kids gets lost."

"Also, from time to time I'll have guests. When that happens I'll expect you to remain out of sight."

Guests, hmm? Of the female variety, she supposed. That, too, made her blush because she couldn't imagine what she'd do if she stumbled upon a naked guest.

"And I don't think I need to remind you to keep…" He looked up at her. "What are their names?"

"Samantha and T.J. We call her Sam for short."

"Please keep Sam and T.J. out of my house. Unless there's an emergency."

"They were already told, but I'll remind them."

"And I should probably meet them. Bring them by tomorrow."

Without thinking, she saluted. His brows lifted. She smiled. He stared at her again, a long, drawn-out stare that made her uncomfortable.

"So that's it for yesterday's list. Do what you can with today's to-do list. It should be self-explanatory. You can add calling Claire and asking her if she'll help you with that dog." He stood. "Let me know what she says."

"What about cooking for you?" She tried not to fidget as she stood in front of him. "I have to confess, I'm dying to use that oven."

He appeared to consider her words. "You won't have to cook for me much. I like to graze more than eat big meals."

"Not ever?" She couldn't contain her disappointment.

"And when I do cook, I actually enjoy cooking myself."

Once again, her mouth went slack. "Really?"

And there it was again: the soft chuff. Definitely laughter.

"Yes, really."

"So I guess it's back to my hidey-hole then."

"Let me know how it goes."

She nodded, resisted the urge to smile one last time, then turned and walked away, but as she traveled across the cavernous width of his office, her tennis shoes making nary a sound on the hardwood floors, she had the strangest sensation. He watched her. She was so sure of it that she paused at the doorway, glanced back.

Their gazes connected.

She froze. She wasn't sure why. It was the look on his face. It wasn't one that made her think he was attracted to her in any way shape or form. To be honest, she'd been on the receiving end of those looks more than once since Trev had died. No, it was more like she was a weed he'd spotted in the fancy hedges outside.

Her lips lifted in an automatic smile. He didn't smile back. She turned her smile up to its full wattage. Still no response. Good heavens. The man had the personality of a wooden stick.

"See you later."

And then he did something she didn't expect. He saluted to her. It made her laugh. She didn't know why, but it did, and she didn't mind letting him hear it as she walked toward the stairs.

Chapter Four

She'd laughed at him.

It bothered him. Actually, a lot of things about her bothered him. Her looks affected him in a way he didn't want to admit. The thought of her washing his undergarments had filled him with mild horror, and yet before he'd met her he'd planned for his new housekeeper to do exactly that. Now…?

He was so deep in thought about her that he jumped when his phone chimed. Incoming call from a number he didn't recognize.

"My kids didn't have any luck finding the dog," said a deeply Southern voice. "So I called Claire and she's on her way over with a trap. She thinks we'll have no problem, but we both agree he's not going to a shelter."

He just shook his head, not that Naomi could see it. "Fine. You catch him. You deal with him."

"Sounds good. I told her to meet us out front."

"Us?"

"I presumed you'd want a say in where we place the trap."

She had a point.

But it wasn't until he was outside, watching her round the corner of his house, that he admitted he'd been kidding himself. He could have left the matter to Claire. She was the professional dog handler. But he'd wanted to see Naomi. Had wanted to look for that mischievous grin of hers again.

Why?

It alarmed him, the realization that he was attracted to her.

Claire wasn't there yet, but Naomi spotted him sitting on the porch, the maroon cushions beneath him not the least bit comfortable. He really would need to do something about his furniture. He couldn't have guests over and have them sit on… What was it she'd called it? Medieval torture devices.

"My kids are bummed they won't get to catch Tramp."

She smiled in amusement and it brightened her face in a way that made him want to… He frowned. He didn't know what it made him want to do.

She crossed in front of him, a hint of vanilla trailing in her wake, and sat on the matching redwood seat.

"Ugh." Her smile faltered, but only a little. "Did they use rocks for stuffing?"

"It's the buttons," he said, shifting in his own seat.

She leaned over, her long red hair swinging

forward. It was later in the day now and the sun loved the color. It set the strands afire in such a way that he knew it was natural. All of her was natural, from the dark brows to the thick lashes to the bee-stung lips.

"You mind me asking who decorated? I might hire them to make furniture for my kids to sit in when they're bad."

Almost, *almost*, he laughed. He caught it just in time. He didn't want her to know how easily she charmed him, not since they'd be working so closely together. "You might be onto something."

She straightened suddenly, and he realized a white van was coming down his long drive. They had an uninterrupted view of the land. He'd planned it that way. In his line of business, you always used the terrain to your advantage. Nestled up against a hill, it wouldn't be easy to breach his home from the back, just the front, and he'd helped mitigate the weakness by clearing his property so that only oak trees remained. No shrubs for people to hide behind. Not that he expected enemies. Still, it was always good to be prepared.

"Claire," Naomi said, standing and already on the move.

He'd somehow forgotten that they knew each other. Although Ethan had recommended her for the job, it was clear she'd formed a bond with the man's wife based on the way she ran to Claire's vehicle, her image reflected back to him on its surface.

"That was quick," he heard Naomi say as Claire exited the van.

"I only live half a mile away," Claire said.

The two women hugged and drew back, and Jax realized he'd never seen Claire smile before. Not truly smile. The grin she gave Naomi could have beamed signals up to the moon. They both turned and started walking toward him.

"Are you and the kids settling in okay?"

Naomi nodded. "The kids were all over the place this morning looking for the dog. T.J. said he had a blast. Even Sam seemed to have enjoyed herself. The fresh air is probably good for them."

"I can't wait to meet them. And to see Janus."

"You will. We can all have lunch together."

"Perfect."

Naomi's face was an entire movie cast of emotions, Jax realized, and he couldn't look away. Everything she felt showed. Perhaps that was what fascinated him. In his line of work you never let anyone see what you were thinking. Naomi let it all hang out.

"So you found a dog," Claire said when she made it to the porch, her own ink-black hair loose around her shoulders. Up until he'd met Naomi, he'd thought Claire had the brightest blue eyes he'd ever seen. Now he realized they hadn't even touched the surface.

"He was on the front porch when I got here yesterday."

"And you tried to catch him."

"Actually, no. I thought he belonged to Jax." She glanced at him, smiling. "It was only later that I realized my mistake, and when we tried to catch him earlier, he ran away."

Jax stood, and he didn't hesitate to open his arms. Ethan's wife was petite as a butterfly, but she had the strength of an armored truck. Her son, Adam, had been diagnosed with cancer at a young age. But throughout his many treatments, she'd been there for him, nursing him and caring for him, and you would never have known how sick Adam had been watching him ride around the ranch these days. She'd truly been through hell and come out on the other side and he admired her for it.

"What?" she asked, drawing back. "Tired of chasing bad guys? You have to run off a poor, defenseless dog?"

"It wasn't my fault the dog got away."

"Sure it wasn't."

He just shook his head. "We need to catch it."

"Catch him and feed him and get him cleaned up," Naomi interjected. "Then we'll decide what to do with him."

Jax crossed his arms in front of him. She stared right back, not backing down. It made him want to kiss the defiance right off her—

Whoa.

What?

"Okay, you two. Whatever you decide to do, we have to get the dog first. I'll go get the trap, show you how to work it."

Naomi was still staring at him. He shifted his gaze to Claire.

"I should fire you," he heard himself say, and it shocked the hell out of him because he'd never, not *ever*, said such a thing to an employee.

"Even if you do, I'm still going to leave here with that dog."

And she would, too. They stared at each other, Naomi's jaw thrust forward in what he'd come to realize was stubborn defiance. Yet far from making him mad, it made him want to smile.

His gaze moved to Claire. She stared at the two of them in avid fascination. For some reason he went from amused to uncomfortable.

"Let's go get your trap," he told her.

THEY SET THE trap away from the main house, not that it would work.

"We're not going to catch him this way," Naomi said.

Claire glanced at the house where Jax had disappeared to a few moments ago. "Don't tell *him* that."

They both stood back, staring at the wire cage with a can of cat food on the trigger. "He's the bossiest man I've ever met."

"He has to be in his line of work."

She felt her lips purse. "I guess. But I have to confess, I'm worried about how he'll react to my kids."

"They haven't met?"

"Not really. When we arrived I hid them in the apartment."

Claire smiled. "Trust me. You have nothing to worry about. He has a nephew he adores. I've seen them out together. He's a different man around kids."

"I hope so."

Claire tipped her head. "You still having trouble with Sam?"

Naomi looked away for a moment. "I don't know if it's hormones or if there's something else that has her upset. All I know is the move hasn't helped matters."

"I bet it hasn't. But take heart. There's so much to do here. Once you get her involved in 4-H and the ranch animals, she'll perk up."

"I hope so."

"Maybe I can talk to her. You know, sometimes it's easier to open up to a stranger."

"Not Sam. She's like a clam." Naomi shook her head. "As opposed to T.J. He's an open book."

"It'll be nice to finally meet them."

"I'm sure they'll be grateful for the company. I think they're kind of bored."

"They'll settle in. And when school starts, they'll make friends."

"I hope so. I don't think I could take another year of T.J. being bullied. And his glasses being broken. And being called a nerd and taunted because he's not athletic. Poor kid has been through enough."

Claire's eyes saddened. "You've all been through enough."

And now she was in a new place with a new boss and a new life. Some people might call her crazy. It wasn't that. More like…desperate.

"Come on. I'll introduce you."

But Claire didn't move. "It's going to be okay, you know. The kids will be fine. And Jax might come off as tough, but on the inside he's complete mush."

"I'll take your word for it."

Claire touched her arm in reassurance. "You're going to impress the socks off him."

Impress? Doubtful.

Her friends loved him so he must be a good guy, but she had a feeling he was a workaholic. He would expect a lot and give back all he had in return. But there was something else about him, too. He had a young face, but his eyes… they were old. She'd seen the same kind of eyes on men who'd returned from the Middle East. Trevor had come home looking like that, but she'd always been able to tease a smile back onto his face. Maybe that was why she'd stood her ground with Jax. He reminded her of Trevor, and she'd automatically reverted to form. Goading him into laughter. Saying whatever thing came to mind. Making him smile until the kind-hearted Jax made an appearance.

She couldn't decide if that was good or bad.

Chapter Five

"Do you think I'll get to ride a horse soon?"

Naomi pulled the covers up to T.J.'s chin. Her big ten-year-old. Never too old to have her tuck him in at night.

"I think it's possible. I'll talk to him about it in the morning."

T.J.'s warm hand fell on her own. His eyes earnest. "You like him, don't you, Mom?"

She leaned toward him. "Of course I do."

She'd spent the day working her tail off for the man, but she supposed that was a good thing

because it kept her mind off the move and wor-
rying about her kids. After she'd finished, she
spent the rest of the evening unpacking their
clothes and tidying the apartment.

"Is he nice?"

"He is."

She'd stood up to him about Tramp, and rather
than get angry, he'd let her have her way. In
hindsight, she probably should have kept her
mouth shut. Too much was riding on this to
blow it with her new boss.

"Do you think I'll ever get to see the inside
of his house?"

"Of course you will."

Please keep Sam and T.J. out of my house.

His words made her bite back a frown. She
didn't blame the man. She really didn't. But that
was the problem. One minute he let her tease
him. The next he was so stern. Such a contradiction.

"I wish I didn't have to go to school."

The words drew her instantly back to the present. "You have months before you have to worry about that."

Her son fiddled with her fingers. "You think they'll be nicer here?"

She leaned down, touching her nose to his before drawing back. "I know they will."

"Sam won't have any problems." He frowned. "She gets along with everyone. Especially the boys."

And that *was* the problem. She'd noticed Sam was just a little too into some of those boys, especially given her young age. It had scared her. She worried that her daughter was so in need of male attention, she looked for it in the wrong place.

Oh, Trevor. Why'd you have to go and leave us?

As if sensing her thoughts, Janus sat up from his position alongside T.J.'s bed. The dog rarely left the boy's side.

"Sam will need to make new friends, too. And you'll both have all summer to do so. You'll feel better about school once you get to know people."

She squeezed his fingers then leaned down and kissed his forehead. "Sleep tight."

Janus's tail thumped when she rose to leave the room. "Keep the bad dreams away," she told the dog, who lay back down.

She would swear the dog's mouth lifted in a smile. Her husband's dog was the smartest animal she'd ever met. He'd helped T.J. through some rough nights. For whatever reason, her son had nightmares about Trevor's death and Janus seemed to sense them. They'd gotten better with time, probably in part because of Janus, but every once in a while they would strike. And it broke her heart.

The sheen of her son's tablet screen caught her eye. It sat on his night table, a piece of furniture that had probably cost as much as her truck. The whole place was decorated with finely crafted pieces that she worried incessantly about her kids scratching.

"Good night," she told her son, and then, before she could think better of it, grabbed the tablet. It was part of the mom code that your kids got all the fancy electronics before you did. T.J. used it to read books and play games and watch videos. But it had internet.

You shouldn't.

She wanted to. She couldn't deny it. She wanted to know more about Jaxton Stone.

She passed Sam's room. Another perk of the job. Her daughter had her own space now, too, instead of sharing a room with T.J., not that she seemed to care. She didn't even look up as Naomi passed by. Too busy reading a book, and to be honest, Naomi was glad. Better that than texting her friends or being online and maybe meeting some boy that was really a perverted old man. She hated the internet and the trouble her kids could get into. Too much surfing could lead to trouble.

Like you're about to surf?

Yeah? So what, she told herself, settling down on a plush couch. She tried entering his name first, surprised when his picture and bio came right up. It was just a snip from his website. Darkhorse Tactical Solutions, or DTS. She clicked on the full link.

Founded nearly two decades ago, Darkhorse Tactical Solutions (DTS) owes its success to Jaxton Stone. A former MI (Military Intelligence) specialist for the Army, he holds a PhD in strategic management and a BA in political science. One of the youngest owners of a military contracting firm, Mr. Stone brings a unique blend of experience to DTS, one gained while serving three tours in the Middle East. He speaks three languages, is highly decorated, and prides himself on putting the safety and security of his clients on the same level as those he employs.

She leaned back. Three tours. That was a lot of time spent overseas. Now that she thought about it, that explained the stony appearance. He'd learned it from the military, where you were taught to keep your thoughts from showing on your face.

She clicked on the DTS homepage. There was a picture of men in camo with the desert as a backdrop. It took her a moment to realize that the man in the middle, the one with dark protective glasses and at least three days' growth of beard, was Jax. He was younger, and he held some type of assault rifle, but she recognized the stern expression on his face. The caption read, "Jaxton Stone, Founder (middle)."

She studied him. It made her wonder what he'd been through. What he'd seen. Based on what she'd learned from Trevor, none of it had probably been good. But he was single. How much harder would it be to bear the burdens of your terrors when there was nobody to lean on once you came back home? Maybe that was why he'd started his security firm. Maybe he'd needed to surround himself with men who understood.

She set the tablet down. She had no doubt Jax was a nice man. He clearly had a code of ethics, too. You didn't get medals from the Army unless you did something pretty spectacular. But rather than reassure her, the realization that she worked for a man a lot like Trevor unnerved her. Most of the men she'd met since Trevor's death were ordinary and uninteresting. Jaxton Stone definitely wasn't that.

War hero.

A man who didn't brag about his accomplishments or display them in any way. A man who gave one-hundred percent of his time and effort to the company he ran and the men who worked for him. He would be a fantastic boss. She should consider herself lucky to have gotten a job with him, especially one that included lodging and a fancy ranch for her kids to enjoy.

She nibbled on a nail. She needed to put aside her concerns. From here on out she would focus on the positives, not the negatives. She would be the best damn employee Jaxton Stone had ever seen. When she was done planning this party, he'd wonder what he ever did without her.

JAX WONDERED IF he should have hired her.

The next morning he found himself staring out the windows of his office again, thinking he could probably hire an outside housekeeper, one who didn't come with kids and a dog and a pair of stunning blue eyes. He could outsource the event planning to his main office. It might make things a little difficult, but it could be managed.

And then she'd be without a job. And homeless. And in a strange state.

The thought had him spinning to face his computer. He should focus on work, so he shot off a quick email to his IT guy, asking if her laptop had been delivered yesterday. Brady's response was nearly instantaneous. It would arrive today, and there was an apology for the delay. That was how Jax operated. Quickly. Efficiently. Fluidly. He was so involved in shuffling through emails and fielding phone calls that he hardly spared a thought for the delivery truck that came and went. Jax knew she was on his network when a chat box suddenly appeared.

Hey there, boss.

He hesitated a moment. If he replied it might open up a conversation, and he really didn't need that right now. He was in the middle of a sensitive negotiation between an Israeli business mogul who needed security for his wife when she came stateside for a few weeks. The man might be richer than Croesus, but he always drove a hard bargain, which was probably how he got to be so rich. Drove him nuts.

I see you received your laptop.

He'd typed without thinking, his fingers flying across the keyboard before he could stop himself, and damned if he knew why.

The software told him she was typing, and he found himself holding his breath as he waited for her reply.

I did, but it's like driving a new car. I don't know where anything is and I keep waiting to crash it.

He smiled, glanced at his email inbox, thinking Yosef might have responded. He hadn't and so he typed:

You found the chat icon quickly enough.

That's because I love to talk.

He sensed that to be true. He'd watched her standing outside with Claire earlier, talking animatedly.

Hello? she typed.

At least you can admit your faults.

Ouch.

He'd been teasing a bit, unusual for him. But, of course, she didn't know that. Don't worry. I'm used to it. My sister could talk the ears off a marble bust.

Your sister is adorable.

On that they could agree. Still, he couldn't help but type: You wouldn't say that if you were helping to plan her wedding.

I would LOVE to help her plan her wedding.

You're hired then.

He'd been half joking, but once he typed the words he realized Naomi might not want to add to her already huge to-do list.

Do you mean it?

Twenty-four hours ago he would have added to her workload without a second thought. He gave a lot to his employees, but he expected a lot, too. Suddenly he wondered if sometimes he asked too much.

Only if you want to.

Her response was immediate. I do!

He nodded even though she couldn't see it. I'll check with Lauren then and see if she minds.

Got it, boss.

She didn't say anything further, and anyway, his email binged and he saw at once it was Yosef, but it surprised him how much he wanted to go on chatting with her. Instead, he busied himself with more work, checking in with his men in the field. There were new contracts to assign. Jobs to be billed. He had a host of staff in the Bay Area, but he kept an eagle eye on things because that was just his way.

Control freak, his sister said. Obsessive, some of his employees claimed. He called it detail-oriented, and in his line of work that could save your life.

He just hoped he didn't scare Naomi away.

His fingers froze on the keyboard. What an odd thing to think. His management style was to set the tone of employment right from the get-go. Employees either lasted or they didn't. He wanted Naomi to last.

It's because she reminds you of your sister.

Was that it? he asked himself. Or was it really the intense attraction he felt every time she walked into a room?

Whatever he felt, he would keep it under wraps. They both had too much to do to have it any other way.

"KNOCK, KNOCK."

He'd been waiting for those words since he'd first sat down to work this morning. Crazy. And she waltzed in like she owned the place, red hair flying, lips lifted in a smile, a sheaf of papers in her hand.

"My liege," she said with a small bow, but then she straightened a bit and he spotted the hint of color that spread from her neck and up to her cheeks, almost as if she didn't mean to tease him.

"I'm sorry," she said.

Just as he suspected. The words had slipped.

"No. It's okay." He tossed his own sheaf of papers across his desk, the documents sliding for a bit before coming to a stop near the edge. "What do you have for me?"

"A list of potential caterers." She sat down in front of him, and her smile could warm even the hardest of hearts. "Thank you Google and Yelp."

"Are they local?"

She nodded, pushed a lock of her hair behind her ear, revealing the plumpness of her lobe.

Why was he staring at that lobe? Why did he have to force his gaze away? "I figured you'd want to patronize local businesses."

"I do."

"So here's my list. Of them all, I'd recommend Bill's Barbecue. He does a lot of local events. Crowd favorite. Voted Best of Via Del Caballo for five years in a row. For an outdoor event, I think he'd be great. And since you want the event in the arena, I was thinking we could drape a canvas top from the center, sort of like a circus tent, and lay down a portable floor. We could set up an open bar in the grooming stall, let your guests actually interact with the horses. Later we could take them on a tour of the guest apartments above the arena. I think it would be perfect."

It would be perfect. Clearly she understood what he was trying to accomplish. He wanted to show off the facility, yes, but he also wanted to make a statement. Local brass needed to understand that he was utterly committed to making Dark Horse Ranch one of the premier therapeutic ranches in the nation. Holding the event down at the arena was a masterstroke. People could see firsthand what he had to offer.

"Book the caterer," he said. "Reserve the tent or whatever you plan to put in the center of the arena. And the tables and chairs. Everything you need—you have some excellent ideas."

She beamed. "Far out. I'll get on it right away."

Far out?

He shook his head, and that's when he saw it. On the screen to his left was the image of a dog, one that stood on his front porch, eating out of a can of…cat food.

"Son of a—" He stood abruptly.

"What?"

"He's back." He pointed to his computer screen.

"Who?"

"That damn dog."

She stood up, leaning toward him, the scent of her catching his attention. He actually had to close his eyes.

"He's got the cat food." She drew back. Thank goodness she moved away. "The little sucker outsmarted the cage."

"Clearly." He stood, started to head for the door.

She beat him to it, blocking his way. "No," she said, holding out her free hand and pressing it against his chest.

He froze.

She did, too.

Her hand. He stared at it for a moment, shocked. None of his other employees had ever dared to touch him in the past. Okay, they'd shaken his hand, but it wasn't just that she actually touched his person. No. Her fingers were soft and petite and so warm.

"I'm sorry," she said for the second time that morning.

I'm not.

The words were on the tip of his tongue, hovering there, about to jump off, but he talked them back from the edge, reminded himself that she worked for him.

"I wasn't going to try to run him off," and even to his ears the words sounded strained.

"I know that, but we have to do this carefully so we don't startle him."

She looked up at him so imploringly, her blue eyes the color of butterflies. She reminded him of the beautiful creatures. Someone who might fly away at the slightest touch.

Whoa, whoa, whoa. Where had that thought come from?

"What do you suggest?"

"I'll go out first, from my apartment, walk up to him slowly. He's met me before, so he won't be scared. I'll catch him somehow and we'll bring him inside."

"Good plan."

She smiled, and it was like dropping off the edge of a building. His head swam for a moment and he had to resist the urge to take a step back.

"I'll grab one of Janus's leads on my way through the apartment," she said.

Why did he react so strongly to her smiles? What was wrong with him?

She left in a hurry. He followed, and much to his chagrin, caught himself glancing down at her backside. She wore a white long-sleeved shirt, and her jeans sparkled with rhinestones. That was what caught his eye.

At least, that was what he told himself.

"You stay here," she ordered, and then the smile notched up a degree. "Be ve-wee, ve-wee qwiet," she whispered in an Elmer Fudd voice. "Whee'rhuntin'wabbits."

Her lips twitched, laughter hovering just at the edge of her mouth and, damn, she did it for him.

He wanted to kiss her.

She turned just in time, because had she been

staring at his face, she might have caught the way he swiped a hand over it. Might have seen the way he turned away from her, reeling.

He desired her.

There was just one problem. She still wore a ring on her finger. Clearly, she still had a thing for her husband. He doubted she was the type to have an affair with her boss, too. And the fact that he was even thinking that scared the crap out of him.

Get a grip, Stone.

She was just a woman. A very pretty woman. He'd faced far more serious threats to his peace of mind. Hadn't he?

THERE WAS SOMETHING fundamentally wrong with having to sneak up on a dog. It didn't help that her kids had begged and pleaded to help out on her way through the apartment. Naomi slowly rounded the edge of the house, glancing back just in case her kids decided to ignore her order to stay inside. Only as she turned the corner did she realize she needn't have bothered sneaking up on Tramp. He'd known she was there. The moment she peeked around the edge of the porch, he tilted his head, eyes shooting right to her.

Well, alrighty then.

"Hey there, boy," she crooned.

Through one of the tall windows she spotted Jax. He stared down at her in a way that made her skin tingle, although why that was, she had no idea. He was just watching her. At least he'd done as she'd asked and stayed put. Tramp seemed to be responding well to her presence. He hadn't fled, not even when she took a step toward him.

"Don't run away," she said softly.

He bolted—right for her.

What?

One minute she was standing, the next she was on her butt and being licked to death.

"Tramp. No." Which came out sounding like, "Trampth. Noth."

"Naomi," someone yelled. Jax, concern evident in his voice.

"It's okay." She grabbed Tramp by the collar, clipped the leash to it. "I'm all right."

She looked up, froze. He stared down at her, and there was such a look on his face, one she didn't immediately recognize.

Possessiveness.

She leaned back in surprise. "I'm fine," she gasped out.

He was probably just protective by nature. There was no reason for him to stare down at her possessively. He was her boss, not a boyfriend.

She blushed at the thought of *that* ever happening.

Tramp realized there was another human there and decided to check him out in the same way he'd checked her out—by jumping up on him.

"Down," he ordered as she scrambled to her feet. Her butt throbbed. The cheeks on her face had warmed, too. She decided to avoid eye contact. Clearly she was reading things on his face that weren't there.

"Let's get him inside before he slips his collar," he said.

"Good idea."

But they had to half drag, half lead him there. When they made it to the porch, his claws skittered across the surface, as if digging into the wood could stop his progression forward. In the end Jax had to push on his rear end to get him through the door—just in the nick of time, too, because he slipped his collar the moment the door closed behind him.

"Tramp, stay." But the dog bolted. "No!" Naomi cried as Tramp jumped up on Jax's fifty-thousand-dollar couch.

"Down," Jax ordered next.

The command worked, but the way the dog

came at them was all wrong. He used a side table as a springboard. A glass lamp ended up a casualty.

"Hey," she cried again, charging toward the wayward dog. Jax did the same thing. They nearly bumped heads before they both drew apart in surprise. Another crash. A statue had fallen over, one she hadn't even seen before. Another moment where they both ran toward the dog. Tramp didn't notice and didn't care. He had the biggest canine grin on his face she'd ever seen. Considering he hadn't wanted to enter the house, it surprised her. It was as if he'd spied that sofa from outside the house and determined that one day he'd use it for a doggy trampoline.

"Grab him," Jax ordered.

She was trying, but he slipped her grasp. She straightened up and yelled at the top of her voice, "Tramp!"

To her absolute and utter shock, the dog slid

to a stop, turned and headed right for her. She could read the intent in his eyes.

"No." She held her hand out.

Jax took the blow in her stead. One moment he stood behind her, the next he was in front of her and Tramp was rearing back, and they were like two objects colliding at the speed of light, their impact a big bang of canine tomfoolery.

"Jax!" she heard herself cry, for some insane reason trying to catch him. It didn't work. The weight of them all was too much. Jax took the brunt of it. She fell hard, too. Tramp seemed to think it all good fun because he bounced up and down on them both, pink tongue hanging out, muddy paws leaving prints on her shirt.

"Sit!" Jax yelled.

Tramp sat.

It was like the moment after a bomb blast. The instant where all was quiet and you tried to take stock of what'd just happened.

"He knows sit," she said in awe.

"Clearly he does."

"And you thought he'd been dumped."

"Clearly he was, and probably because he doesn't listen."

Tramp just looked at them both, happiness shining from his eyes, and Naomi started to laugh. She couldn't help it. Here she was in one of the most prestigious and most gorgeous homes she'd ever seen, and one four-legged canine had managed to ruin it all. Well, just the living room.

She expected Jax to sit up, to scowl, to frown at her in a "see, I told you so" sort of way. Instead he tipped his head so they were eye to eye, and her whole world tumbled end over end because of the look on his face. She could have sworn she saw his gaze dart to her lips, but he pulled it back again and her own humor faded as her heart began to *thu-dump, thu-dump, thu-dump* in her ears.

"You okay?" he asked gently.

No. She wasn't okay. Not at all. Her heart pounded. Her skin tingled. Her chest rose and fell.

"Yeah, I'm good."

His gaze dropped to her lips again. She looked at his lips, too, and then he rolled toward her and she could feel his breath on her face and she thought he might… That he could possibly… That she wanted him to…

He got up.

If she'd been a candle she would have melted at his feet. He waved a warning hand at Tramp. She forced herself to breathe.

He held out a hand. "Now that we've got him, what are we going to do with him?"

"A bath." Her lips trembled. "I'll have the kids give him a bath."

He stared down at her, hand outstretched, and she stared at his masculine fingers and wondered if she had the courage to clasp them.

Tramp took the decision out of her hands,

shooting toward her and sliding his tongue across her face.

"Hey," she cried, sitting up. Somewhere, almost out of the range of her hearing, she thought she heard him say, "Lucky dog."

Chapter Six

He'd damn near kissed her.

Jax tried not to think about that as they headed toward the door to her apartment. Okay, more like forcibly pushed the almost-kiss from his mind.

"Did you catch him?"

The words were said by an exuberant little boy who'd clearly been waiting for them. T.J.'s eyes fell on the dog behind them. "Cool!"

"Where's Janus?" Naomi asked.

"In the front, staring out the window," T.J.

said, half turning. "Janus, *bliff*." He brought his hand to his chest to emphasize the German command because clearly Janus wasn't at the window anymore. The dog stopped in his tracks, but Tramp had caught sight of him and in a matter of seconds he was at the end of the leash, whining, crying, barking. Janus didn't move, a testament to his military training.

"This isn't going to work." Naomi's daughter had to yell to be heard. "You can't just bring a strange dog in here, Mom."

She was right.

"You can give him a bath in my tub," Jax offered.

"Really?" the little boy said.

"Tramp, come," he ordered, pulling the dog back. The crazy canine didn't want to listen again, furthering his suspicion that lack of self-control was clearly why he'd been dumped in the country.

"Come on, Tramp," Naomi said.

Somehow they managed to drag and pull Tramp back into Jax's home. When they closed the door, he settled down a bit, but only a bit.

"I'm T.J., by the way," said the little boy, his glasses reflecting the light of the kitchen window.

"Nice to meet you, T.J."

"This place is amazing," he said, staring around him in awe.

"Should we give him a bath in here?" Naomi asked.

"I doubt we'll be able to get him near a sink. Probably best to use the tub in my bedroom."

"Cool!" T.J. cried. "I get to see your house."

The boy reminded him of his nephew, especially when he raced toward the entrance to the kitchen. Tramp clearly wanted to join him, because it took everything Jax had to stop the leash from sliding through his fingers.

"Wow," the boy said, staring around him, mouth slightly open.

"Nice, isn't it?" his mom asked.

Did he need a better reason to keep his eyes and hands to himself? Jax wondered. She was a mom. His employee. He shouldn't be staring at her lips and wondering what they might taste like.

"Head up the stairs," he told T.J. Actually, it was good to have the boy out in front of him. Tramp clearly wanted to meet him, because he eagerly followed in his wake. "Head left at the top."

But T.J. had stopped on the landing, peering down below him and into his living room. "This is like the Stark mansion."

Naomi laughed, glanced up at him. "If you knew how much he was into comic books, you'd know that's the biggest compliment he can give."

Tramp was finally able to sniff the boy. T.J. pulled his gaze away from the interior of his house and squatted down. "Hey there, boy."

Yup. Just like his nephew. The same soft touch with animals. The same enthusiastic smile. The same zest for life.

"I'll take him," T.J. said, looking up at Jax.

"No, that's okay," Naomi said. "Let Jax do it, Teej. He can be a lot to handle."

"Awww," the boy said, but then he straightened up and clapped his thigh. "Come on, boy."

And that's how Jax found himself directing everyone into his bedroom, although why he suddenly felt self-conscious about a room Naomi would one day clean, if she hadn't already, he had no idea. He walked past them and opened the bathroom door. Tramp didn't follow; he realized why when he turned back. Both Naomi and T.J. stared around his bedroom in awe, and Tramp refused to budge.

"This is unbelievable." T.J.'s gaze caught on his massive bed. Jax's gaze caught on it, too, but for a whole other reason. And that made him feel like some sort of disgusting creep because he really shouldn't be wondering what T.J.'s mom thought about the bed. He really shouldn't.

"It's gorgeous." Her Southern accent was seasoned with pleasure.

She liked it. He shouldn't care, but he did.

"I spent a lot of time designing it," he admitted.

His bedroom took up the entire southern side of the house—second floor because he couldn't sleep in a room that was ground level. Too easy to break into. Like the front of his home, each end of the house had peaked roofs, and beneath that, walls of glass. From his vantage point he could see the lake, and way off in the distance, the Reynolds property and the glint of a metal roof that was Natalie's covered arena. In the winter, when the grass was green and the lake was full, it would be stunning. He wouldn't know, having just moved in at the beginning of spring, but it was something he looked forward to.

"You could see all the way to the beach from here," T.J. said.

He smiled. "Not quite."

Tramp's nails dug into the Berber carpet, making a popping sound as they all three moved toward his bathroom. "All the way at the end, to the left."

He made the mistake of looking at Naomi, and he saw that she stared at his king-size bed. She must have sensed his gaze, because she half turned and then her body twitched as if it was a physical shock to catch him watching her.

"It's big," she said, and there it was again. The hint of color at her neck. It once again spread up into her cheeks. "You could fit a football team in it," he thought he heard her murmur. But there was admiration on her face and in her voice, and it pleased him.

His bedroom, of all rooms, was the most "him." He might not have been born on a ranch, but he was a cowboy at heart. He'd always been drawn to horses. As a kid he'd watched every old Western movie he could get his hands on, usually starring John Wayne. In hindsight that was probably why he'd joined the military. He was a good guy chasing down bad guys. This ranch was a way of letting the cowboy side of him show through, and so the walls were the same redwood as outside. In front of the tall windows opposite his bed were comfy beige chairs with separate footrests in front. He'd positioned them near enough to the cobblestoned fireplace in the left corner of the room that in the winter he'd be able to feel the warmth of the flames. He saw her gaze catch on the wrought iron light fixture that he'd bought from an old saloon. Some nights he'd stare up at the thing and wonder about all the people who'd stood beneath it over the years.

"It's like a hotel," T.J. said, once again coming to a stop.

"You like it?" he found himself asking.

"I do," T.J. answered, but it was Naomi that Jax watched.

"It's beautiful," she said. "But are you sure about this?" She motioned toward his bathroom.

"It'll be fine." He led the way. Here the granite floors were rough, not polished smooth, and rust and brown in color. A square piece of off-white carpet sat in front of the double vanity, and it was the rug she stared at.

"Holy guacamole," T.J. said. "That's not a bathtub. That's a swimming pool."

Naomi seemed equally shell-shocked. "What if he tries to jump out the window?"

Around the tub they'd used stained glass for privacy—horses against a blue backdrop in a field of gold—and it was, quite frankly, his favorite feature of the house. "He won't jump out of that."

The look she shot him said, "Famous last words," and then she glanced back at the tub again. "All right, T.J. You're going in there with him."

"Cool."

"Although you might need a lifejacket," he heard her mumble.

"Should I get naked?"

"T.J. No." Naomi shot him a look of horrified amusement. "Just roll your pants up."

Tramp, by now, sensed his impending doom. The dog had put on the brakes, despite the sight of his favorite new human climbing into his tub, sans shoes, jeans rolled up. He tried to skitter back toward the door.

"How do you turn the water on?" T.J. asked.

He didn't blame him for asking. He'd had the same reaction when he'd seen the stainless steel fixture shaped like a Santa sleigh. There were no knobs.

"It's all done with a remote control." He pointed toward the edge of the triangular-shaped tub. "The buttons at the top are hot and cold."

"I'll do it," Naomi said. "You try to get Tramp in the tub."

That ought to be interesting.

"He's shaking." T.J. had to raise his voice over the sound of the running water. "I think he knows what's coming."

"I think so, too," Naomi said.

That made three of them. Sure enough, the moment he tried to wrap his arms around the dog's midsection, he bolted for the door.

"Tramp!" Naomi cried.

Jax reached for him as he tried to shoot by. Somehow, he didn't know how, he caught him midstride.

"Come on, boy. This is for your own good." Dog paws waved in the air as if he still tried to run.

"He doesn't think so," she said.

Tramp wanted none of it, and the look on that dog's face… Jax didn't know whether to laugh or pet him. There was such a pathetic expression of "don't kill me" on his face that he found himself leaning down. "It's okay. No one's going to hurt you."

The dog stared up at him, his big brown eyes shielded by bushy brows that reminded Jax of a walrus.

When he looked up he realized Naomi and T.J. stared at him, the craziest expression on Naomi's face, a smile on T.J.'s.

"I think he likes you," the boy said.

"Come on," he told the dog, heading toward the tub. The dog didn't move. Tramp went slack as Jax lifted him over the edge.

"What about shampoo?" Naomi turned back to the bathroom.

"It's in the dispenser there. It's for human hair, but it'll have to do. You have to pump it."

It wasn't easy to slide the dog into the tub without falling in himself, but it helped that T.J. was inside, waiting.

"Do you have any cups or something we could use to scoop water?" she asked.

"Downstairs," he said. "I'll go get them."

"No. I can do that. I'll see if I can't get Sam up here to help, too."

"Good luck with that," T.J. said, squatting down next to the dog. "Hey, boy," he said gently. "I'm not going to hurt you."

But Tramp eyeballed the liquid that steadily rose. Jax knew it would be a matter of time before he tried to jump out again. "All right. Make room."

"What?" T.J. asked.

"I'm coming in."

He sat on the edge of the tub, pulled off his boots and socks, and rolled up his jeans. For a moment he contemplated changing into a T-shirt, but he didn't want to be right in the middle of changing when Naomi, and maybe even her daughter, came in.

"I hope Tramp appreciates this." He gingerly

stepped into the tub. Honestly, he'd never used it before and Naomi was right. He damn near did need a lifejacket. He understood why Tramp stared up at him in terror. From Tramp's point of view, it probably seemed like a giant crater, one quickly filling up with water.

"Sam will be up in a minute." Naomi drew up short at the sight of him, the arm that held blue plastic cups dropping to her side. Then she smiled again. "Good idea."

"I need a cup, Mom." T.J. held out a hand. Naomi gave the boy one, setting the other one down on the rim.

"I think the water's going to soak my jeans." Jax looked up at Naomi.

She'd begun to roll up the sleeves of her shirt.

"You coming in, too?"

"I think the more we all pitch in, the faster this will get done."

"Good thinking, Mom."

So that's how he ended up holding Tramp's

collar while the two of them scooped water over the dog's back. Good thing, too. The first time they poured water over Tramp's back, the dog lunged, but between them all they managed to keep him inside the tub.

"Okay, what do you need me to do?"

They all three looked toward the bathroom door. Sam stood there, her dark hair pulled into a ponytail, an expression of extreme boredom on her face. She always looked that way, Jax was starting to realize.

"Perfect timing," he heard T.J. say. "Right when we're almost done."

"Shut up, brat," Sam said.

"Towels," Naomi interjected, making him think their verbal warfare was a common occurrence. Distraction was a good technique to head off a fight.

"Where are they?" Sam asked.

"In the cabinet behind you," Jax said.

"I bet this is what the White House looks like," she muttered, turning toward the cabinet.

"Poor guy," Naomi said, ignoring her daughter. "He's been lost a long time. He's so skinny."

And scared. And Jax wouldn't be human if it didn't tug at his heart.

"We'll get him fixed up."

He met her gaze. Their heads were only inches apart, and she smelled like vanilla and lemons again. Moisture clung to her skin, highlighting the striking perfection of it, her lashes so long they nearly touched her eyebrows. Her lips were red and he realized it was because she kept biting them in concentration. He had a hell of a time pulling his gaze away.

"What are you going to do with him once you're done?" Sam asked, having come back with the towel, and there was a look on the girl's face, one that made him feel suddenly self-conscious. He hoped like hell she didn't think he liked her mom or anything, because he didn't. Not like that. "You can't keep him in our place, not with Janus."

"First things first." Naomi blinked at Jax a

few times before looking up at her daughter. "We're going to dry him off. Then we're going to take him for a walk, and after that we'll put him in the laundry room until we're sure he'll get along with Janus."

"Really?" Sam said, and it wasn't a supportive *really*. More like a "good luck with that" really.

"Don't be such a doubting Thomas."

Naomi turned back to him with a smile on her face, her red hair falling over a shoulder, and the look she gave him was full of cheerful optimism. He drew back. God, what was it like to be her? To say it would all work out and to actually believe it? To go into something with such confidence? In his experience things rarely worked out as planned.

"And what about after all that?" her daughter asked.

"We're going to take him to the vet to see if he has a microchip, and then we're going to find his home, either his old one or a new one." She leaned down, lifting the dog's face and asking him, "Okay?"

Tramp bolted.

"No!" she cried, reaching for the leash. It slipped from her grasp.

Jax tried to grab it, too, but the dog scrambled out despite their best efforts. Tramp didn't count on slick paws and a wet floor when he landed. The moment he tried to gain purchase, he slid sideways. Sam reached for him, but Tramp saw her coming and clambered toward the bedroom.

"Get him!" T.J. cried.

All three of them dashed out of the tub, but it was too late. The dog headed for the door like a linebacker on Sunday morning. They should have closed the bathroom door, Jax realized, an oversight on their part because the dog didn't want to stop.

"Darn dog!" Sam yelled, trying to grasp his tail.

They disappeared around the corner and Jax

figured they were doomed. Once the dog spied the open bedroom door he'd make a break for it.

Only…the door wasn't open.

Sam must have closed it on her way through. Tramp ran toward it, stopped, then ducked left. He knew what would come next. Sure enough the dog headed for his bed.

"No!" they all cried.

Too late. Up he went, Sam reaching him first, the girl trying desperately to grab the leash, but his bed was big and the dog was quick. He jumped off the other side and headed back the direction he'd come, spotted the three of them and turned toward his fireplace, hitting the rack that held the tools and scattering them everywhere.

"Get him," Sam ordered.

How one dog evaded them all was anyone's guess, but evade them he did, Tramp dashing around and between and over the bed until they'd covered every square inch of his bedroom more than once. A picture was knocked from the wall. Some books from a shelf. A carpet runner flipped sideways. It wasn't until T.J. dived headfirst onto the bed, Tramp captured beneath him, that they were able to get close. To give the dog credit, he didn't try to snap at the boy, just attempted to wiggle out beneath him.

"I got him," T.J. cried.

Naomi grabbed the end of the leash. Sam grabbed the collar and Tramp looked up at them all, mouth open, eyes wide, his expression clearly asking, "What now?"

Jax almost laughed. Naomi let out a snort and clapped a hand to her mouth, eyes wide. Sam smiled. T.J. started to giggle, too.

He felt an emotion build inside him then, something he hadn't felt since his sister and her son moved out of the house. A kind of satisfaction. He tried to analyze it, couldn't come up with a reason why he felt that way, and so instead he said, "I guess he's dry now."

Which made all three of them laugh, which made the satisfaction turn into something else, something he couldn't identify, and that scared the hell out of him.

Chapter Seven

"He doesn't smile very much."

Naomi kept her gaze on Tramp as they walked toward the horse barns, Samantha's observation having the ring of truth. T.J. had insisted on going for a walk once she was done with work, and she didn't blame him after being cooped up in the apartment all day. She'd made a ton of progress on her to-do list. She'd worked far more than eight hours, popping in to see her kids and check on Tramp throughout the rest of the afternoon. She figured it was the least she could do after completely wrecking Jax's morning with the Tramp Fiasco, as she now called it.

"He's just a very busy man," she said, watching as T.J. rounded the corner with Janus leading the way. The two dogs had met face-to-face, and much to her surprise, Janus seemed unfazed. She would still lock Tramp in the laundry room for now, but at least their first meeting hadn't been a complete disaster. Tomorrow she'd take Tramp to get scanned. Later tonight she'd work on flyers. All in all, a productive day.

"I don't get why you'd want to work with him," Sam said, hands in the pockets of her denim jacket, brown hair in a ponytail. She looked about five years old, but Naomi knew it was just an illusion. Her daughter had slipped right into puberty without her realizing it.

"It's a great job." She'd told Sam that at least a hundred times on the way out. "Not many jobs give you a place to stay for free. Plus a great salary. And it's close enough to Nona and Papa that you can visit them. And I'll have flexible hours. I get to see you guys all the time. It's a win-win."

"Not if your boss is a jerk."

"He's not a jerk." And it surprised her how quickly she came to Jax's defense. Claire had been right. He seemed tough on the outside, but inside was a different story. Look at how he'd jumped in to help with Tramp. For whatever reason, he just liked to keep his emotions to himself.

"He likes you."

That made Naomi stop. "What makes you say that?"

Sam stopped, too. Her blue eyes had the strangest expression in them. "You should have seen the way he was looking at you."

She dismissed her daughter's observation with a swipe of her hand. "He was probably just thinking about what a crazy woman I am for bringing a dog into his house."

"No, Mom." And if Sam had had glasses, she would have been looking over the rim of them. "He was staring at you like you were some kind of giant ice cream cone."

Her cheeks flamed, even though she knew her daughter had to be wrong. Still, just the thought of Jax, maybe, possibly, sort of liking her filled her with an odd sort of glee, an excitement that instantly changed into a massive dose of guilt, or maybe horror. She didn't have feelings about her boss. She almost told Sam that she didn't know what she was talking about, that she was too young to recognize attraction. But these days that type of comment would be the opening salvo to a verbal war, so she kept quiet and decided to change the subject.

"Are you excited about your trip with Nona and Papa?"

"You don't like him back, do you?"

So much for changing the subject. Why did it feel like she was about to tell her daughter a lie? "Of course not. Not like that," she quickly amended. "He's a nice man, but he's my boss. I'm just excited about working for him. It will open so many doors, especially once we sell the house."

Her daughter narrowed her eyes and Naomi wondered what she would do if she ever decided to date someone. She had a feeling Sam would consider it a betrayal of her dad's memory if she took the plunge. Thankfully she had no plans to bring a man into her life anytime soon.

"Will we be able to pet the horses?" T.J. called from up ahead.

They'd rounded the corner of the hill, the arena and pastures spread out in front of them. The fact that neither T.J. nor Sam reacted to the site of the massive structure told her they'd seen it before, not that she was surprised. They'd canvassed a wide area looking for Tramp the other day. She just hoped they'd obeyed her instructions to stay away from the horses.

"Head for the sorrel horse in the pasture."

Her son turned back to her, a puzzled look on his face, and she knew immediately what the problem was. "The brown horse," she said, pointing and holding back a laugh, one that changed to a sigh of near sadness. She loved horses, had missed being around them. A part of her wondered how different life would have been for her kids if her own parents hadn't been taken from her all those years ago. It would have been great if they'd been able to afford one.

T.J. ran off, and Janus instantly matched his steps to her son's. Tramp whined, but she settled him with a pat on the head. She expected Sam to run off, too. Sam was her horse-crazy kid, and yet she stuck by her mother's side. That was part of the reason why she'd decided to move, too, so Sam could get closer to the animals she loved.

"Don't you want to join your brother?"

"In a minute."

Uh-oh.

"We're leaving next week," her daughter said.

"Yeah. Disney World. Are you excited?"

It had been one of the bummers about starting to work in California so soon. She would miss the kids' first trip to the world-renowned amusement park. It was one their grandparents had been planning for nearly a year, but she hadn't wanted to ask for the time off, especially once she'd heard about Jax's party. Though if she were honest, it didn't upset her too much. She and her mother-in-law didn't exactly see eye to eye. It been one of the toughest decisions of her life to follow them to retirement on the West Coast. In the end the fact that the kids only had Trevor's parents left—no aunts or uncles or another set of grandparents, just Rose and Walt—had decided the matter. And then she'd heard about the job less than two hours away from where Rose and Walt had bought a home and it'd seemed like fate.

"I wish you could come, Mom. I just don't like you here all by yourself."

All by herself. As in alone with Jax. That was what this was about.

"I'll be fine."

Sam just stared. Naomi felt heat stain her cheeks once again. "Sam. It's not like that."

She lifted a brow. Behind the bravado, something like worry flitted through her daughter's eyes. "Really?"

"Really," Naomi said emphatically.

"Can I pet him, Mom?"

T.J. stood by Zippy's head, bouncing from foot to foot. Janus stared up at the horse, ears pricked, slightly crouched, as if daring the animal to try to nip his human.

"Go ahead, hon. He won't bite."

They'd passed by the massive riding complex without Naomi noticing. That startled her, but she supposed she'd been pretty deep in thought, still must have been because Sam had hung back, and it took Naomi a second or two to realize it. She stopped and turned back to her daughter, her blue eyes full of some emotion Naomi didn't recognize.

"Do you still love Dad?"

The question took her by such surprise it literally robbed her of breath. "Of course I do, honey."

Sam's gaze scanned her face as thoroughly as an FBI agent. "Do you miss him?"

"More than you know."

At last the fear in her daughter's eyes started to fade away. Satisfied, Sam turned to the horse, and Naomi was pleased to note the interest in her eyes. She watched as she tentatively approached the animal, but it was Naomi's turn to hang back.

Her daughter's question hadn't been random. She'd asked because she was afraid she might be ready to move on with her life. It was the first time Sam had ever done something like that and it made Naomi realize when the time came, if it ever came, she would have to give her kids a heads-up.

But it wouldn't come to that. Not for a long time.

IT WAS THE smell that caught his attention.

It'd been a restless night, and as always happened when he couldn't sleep, he buried himself in his work. He'd spent the entire night getting caught up, although that was nearly impossible to do given how many clients he had overseas, but he knew the day would come when he'd have to leave the peace and sanctity of his ranch. Some things, like hiring new employees and soliciting new clients, simply couldn't be done from home.

But that smell…it was like something from his past. He couldn't put his finger on it until he followed his nose out of his office and down the staircase. He heard music, a frisky beat that he recognized as a current hit. His nose led him into his kitchen, and Jax stopped in his tracks at the sight and smells that greeted him.

"There you are," Naomi said in her Deep South drawl. "I was wondering if I'd manage to lure you down."

"You're cooking."

Her smile could have charmed birds from a tree. "I sure am." She pointed with a pair of tongs toward the center island that he rarely—come to think of it, that he'd never—used. She'd put down placemats and kitchen crockery that his designer had picked out for him months ago.

She smiled. "Already cooked my little ones their own breakfast. No big deal to come over here and do the same."

"I told you it wasn't necessary to cook me meals."

Her smile slipped just a little bit. "You did,

but you've been working so hard up there, I doubt you even thought about eating. Go on." She clacked her tongs together, pointing toward a bar stool.

He didn't want to. He really didn't. But he also didn't want to see that smile fade, because she looked adorable standing there in a denim button-down shirt that'd been rolled up at the sleeves and a white apron tied behind her. She'd piled her thick red hair atop her head in such a way that it seemed ready to tip off the side, yet it somehow stayed in place as she opened the oven and grabbed…

Waffles. He loved waffles.

"Where's Tramp?"

"I'm still keeping him in the laundry room for now. He met Janus last night, but you never know. The kids already walked and watered him. I called Claire. I'm going to take him into the Via Del Caballo Animal Clinic later today."

He sat down. She placed the tray of waffles

down in front of him and he realized that was what he'd smelled. Sugar and flour and eggs.

"I figured we could make this a working breakfast seein' as how I know how hard it is for you to pull yourself away from your desk." She grabbed a spatula.

And God help him, the smell of those waffles made his stomach growl. She had bacon, too. He saw that when she put another plate down. And a bowl of freshly cut fruit, although where she'd gotten it he had no idea. And what appeared to be warmed-up maple syrup.

"Want some OJ?" she asked, grabbing a pitcher. She poured him a glass without waiting for an answer, then leaned her elbows on the counter and waited for him to take a bite, her brows lifted in anticipation, the look on her face one that told him how much she enjoyed cooking and how much she looked forward to seeing his reaction to her food.

He took a bite. Soft, fluffy waffle melted in his mouth and he very nearly groaned.

"Good?" she asked.

He nodded because, honestly, he didn't want to waste time talking. Only then did he admit how famished he was and how much he needed to eat, and so he did. Naomi stood across the counter from him, resting her chin on her palms, her smile getting bigger and bigger as he wolfed down the first waffle. She served him another one without asking. This time, however, she grabbed a sheet of paper from the counter behind her after she'd served him.

"Okay." She grabbed a pen from a cup he didn't remember having, but that she'd clearly found somewhere and placed on the center island. "So I've booked the barbecue guy." He watched her tick off an item while he kept on eating. "He's not cheap, but what are you going to do? I've also taken the liberty of hiring a band. I know, I know, I probably should have consulted you, but in the interest of saving time, I just did it." She peeked up at him. "I hope you don't mind heavy metal."

He nearly choked. She laughed and he stopped chewing because, damn, she was beautiful. Even with her hair hanging haphazardly off her head and wearing a baggy shirt and that white apron, her beauty couldn't be denied.

"I spent yesterday afternoon calling every local politician I could get a hold of. Well, their secretaries and whatnot. And then I called the town mayor. And the local sheriff, who I understand you know, and who said he'd be happy to attend. So far I have forty people attending—"

Forty?

"—and probably more by the time it's all said and done. Your new hippotherapist, for one. And the ranch manager, who are both arriving the same week." She checked off another item.

She set the paper down. "I was thinking maybe we should offer horse rides to your guests? I mean, the goal is to get people talking about Hooves for Heroes, yes? It'd make for some good press to take pictures of people on horseback, especially the non-horsey type. Heck, we might even score some national coverage. And I think the politicians would be more apt to remember your program the next time they're considering a VA bill if we showed them a good time, so an open bar for sure. Might need to get them liquored up to get them on a horse."

He set his fork down, leaned back, and he had to admit it. She'd impressed the hell out of him. Not only with her cooking, but with her smarts.

"The big top will arrive at 0700 next Saturday. It'll be a circus theme. I'm going to hire extras, too. You know, clowns with top hats and super-long ties, maybe some acrobats. I think it'll be fun and different from the usual rodeo-themed events Claire tells me are popular around here."

She met his gaze. "So I ordered invitations, put a rush on them because we're so short on time. I mean, in reality, we should take a few months to plan this event, but it is what it is so I'm taking the plunge and moving ahead at light speed. Hope that's okay."

He took a sip of his orange juice. She'd really taken the ball and run with it. "Talk to our new ranch manager about the guest rides. It's a brilliant idea."

Her eyes lit up.

"It's all great. Better than I could've managed in such a short amount of time."

"Thank you."

Something about her smile filled him with an emotion he couldn't identify, not at first. But then he had it. Pleasure. He liked seeing that grin.

He grabbed his plate. "I'm done."

"I'll take that."

"You don't have to." He headed toward the sink.

"Actually, it's my job."

Yes, it was, but it made him feel somehow rude not to pick up his own plate. Frankly, it made him feel odd to think of her cleaning his house, too. He didn't have time to analyze that, though. Just as he didn't want to analyze why pleasing her pleased him.

"Listen, I wanted to ask you something."

The tone of her voice caught his attention. He turned back from the sink, leaned against it. She did the same thing against the center island, and he could tell from her crossed arms that she was uncomfortable with what she had next.

"I was wondering if my kids could use your pool. I know that's a lot to ask, but T.J.'s been dying to jump in."

"I don't mind them swimming. In fact, my nephew is coming over in a bit to ride horses. Why don't we let them all swim together?"

Her whole face lit up. "That would be great."

And there was the strangest look on her face.

It was as if she'd stepped back and looked at him through a looking glass, and now she saw him differently, and maybe she did see him differently, but then she looked down and the spell was broken.

"I'll go tell them."

"Go on ahead."

She turned and headed back to her apartment and he stared after her. Letting her kids swim was no big deal. It was no more than he would do for any other employee.

That was what he told himself, and man, he almost believed it. The thing was he didn't mind sharing his pool with family. Naomi was an employee, though, and usually he kept a strict line between the people who worked for him and himself. But it wasn't just the thought of breaking his personal employer code that bothered him. It was just the thought of seeing Naomi in a bathing suit that made him wonder if he'd lost his mind.

"UNCLE JAX!"

Kyle scrambled out of his future stepdad's truck faster than a colt coming out of a bucking chute. "I got in. I got in."

There was no sense in asking what he'd gotten into. Since he'd first heard about the junior rodeo state championships, Kyle had one goal in mind—performing there. He'd been carefully tracking his points for two months.

"Way to go, buddy." He gave him a high five. "Go on in and get saddled up while I talk to Bren."

Behind him, Bren Connelly, newly reelected sheriff of Via Del Caballo, got out of his black truck, one with a gold star on the side. He had a teasing grin on his face that told Jax he was about to get seriously hassled by his future brother-in-law.

"So my fiancée tells me she hired you a hot housekeeper."

Just what he expected. Beneath the black cowboy hat, Bren's brown eyes were one-hundred percent fun and games.

"I don't know what you're talking about."

Bren shook his head, stopped beside him, crossed his arms in front of him. "Uh-uh."

Jax tried to sock Bren in the arm, but the man ducked out of the way. "It wouldn't have mattered if she was eighty years old with gray hair. She's perfect for the job."

"Yeah? You let all your employees' kids swim in your pool?"

He'd seen them? Well, of course he had. In Bren's line of work, he would observe things most people wouldn't—like kids swimming in a pool as he drove by—while Kyle probably hadn't noticed a thing. That's what he liked about the man. They were a lot alike, the two of them. His sister couldn't have found a more perfect match for her and her son.

"Her kids are great," Jax said. "I couldn't say no when she asked if they could use the pool."

Bren just gave him a look that said plain as day he didn't believe him.

"Besides, I was thinking Kyle could join them later. He'll be tired after he rides."

Bren considered the words. "So you want me to pick him up this evening?"

He was feeling more and more uncomfortable by the minute. "If that works."

Bren's smile was like a dog that had broken into the food bin. "Well, all right then."

"You don't have to leave right away. I miss the days of riding lessons and beers afterward."

He shook his head. "Kyle told me he can handle it from here on out, and he's right. The kid's a natural."

"He is that."

"Besides, I wouldn't want to intrude on your time with the hot housekeeper."

"Hey, now."

His friend laughed. Jax decided to ignore him.

The more he denied it, the more grief he'd get. Bren was known for his dry sense of humor.

"I'll tell Lauren the plan. You go have fun."

Fun. Yeah. "You sure you don't want to stick around?"

"Nah. I'll leave you alone with the happy homemaker."

He ignored the remark and, a few minutes later, watched Bren drive away. But the whole time he supervised his nephew he couldn't deny the way his heart rate rose and fell in correlation to the direction of his thoughts.

When he slipped through the tall doors of the arena it was in time to see Kyle leading Zippy through the gate. Man, the kid had gotten good. Of course, with jumping lessons and damn near daily riding sessions, he'd had every opportunity to improve. The only rule was that he couldn't ride alone. Someone always had to be nearby in case something happened, and so Jax busied himself around the barn, doing things his friends the Reynoldses had taught him to do: check horse water, clean stalls, give the horses on the ranch the once-over. Right now the horses were all on vacation. That would change soon. Once his therapist and ranch manager arrived they would decide the best course of action on how to get the ranch up and running. Exciting times ahead.

"Uncle Jax, look!"

He glanced through the bars of the horse stall he stood in. He'd built them that way for exactly that reason—so people could watch what was going on in the arena while they worked with the horses. Kyle galloped around the perimeter, Zippy's hooves kicking up dust, the sun catching the particles and turning them into clouds so that it almost appeared as if Kyle flew. The image was helped by the fact that he didn't hold onto the reins. His arms were out to the side and he tipped his head back, laughing, and Jax rested the muck rake in the shavings and just smiled. This. This was why he'd done what he'd done. Why he'd sunk a small fortune into the place. He wanted to bring joy to people's lives. A joy he had yet to find for himself. But that was okay. He could absorb the happiness of others. That was enough for him.

Kyle grabbed the reins again, sat back. Zippy stopped. "That was fun."

"Probably time to call it quits," he said. "If you want to have time to swim before the sun goes down."

Kyle nodded and pointed Zippy toward the stalls. His nephew was still all smiles, sliding expertly to the ground.

"Looks like you're ready for the championship."

Kyle stepped up to the horse's head, clucking to urge Zippy forward. "Bren said it's okay if I get nervous. Everyone has to step up their game, but that all I have to do is put into action everything I've practiced and I'll be fine."

"Are you nervous?"

Kyle stopped. "No. Not really. I don't think so. I get this weird kind of butterfly thing in my tummy when I think about it, but I'm not scared."

"Good for you."

"Come on, Zippy. Time for dinner."

They fed the horse, and it was something Jax planned to keep on doing, even once his ranch manager arrived. There was something about the eager look on a horse's face that always made him smile, and then the calming sound of them munching on food.

"Ready?" he asked when they were finished, glancing back into the empty arena. Soon. Soon all his plans would come to fruition.

"I can't wait to swim."

He realized in that instant why he'd wanted Kyle to join him at the pool so badly. He'd needed a chaperone.

He damn near stumbled.

"You okay, Uncle Jax?"

Jax waved a hand, his heart beating like he'd just run from the barn. He didn't want to be alone with her, although strictly speaking he wouldn't be alone. Her kids would be there, too. And that was part of the problem, as well. For the first time in a very, very long time, he was intimidated, and all by one gorgeous redhead and her two kids.

"Let's go," he told his nephew. Kyle just stared at him strangely, as if he knew something was up, but didn't want to push the matter. He'd always been a smart kid for his age.

"Do you like your new housekeeper?"

He glanced over at his nephew as he started the ATV. At first he thought the kid meant like as in *like*…dating-type like. Then he realized he was just asking in the typical ten-year-old, boys-think-girls-are-yucky type of way.

"She's nice."

And a good cook. And a hard worker. His

house looked spotless. The other day he'd walked into his master bathroom and realized it smelled like vanilla and lemon. He didn't know what it was, but he would bet it was something she'd concocted on her own. Some all-natural, homeopathic cleanser.

"Mom says she's pretty."

She is that. The words were on the tip of his tongue, but he didn't want to admit that to his nephew. All he needed was some form of the comment to be regurgitated later on.

"Nobody is as pretty as your mom."

Kyle nodded in agreement. Jax's hands clenched the steering wheel as they rounded the side of the hill and his house came into view. He could hear a little boy shriek and a dog bark. Tramp appeared to be having the time of his life.

"Is that the dog my mom was telling me about?"

He'd had a conversation with his sister about

Tramp the other night, one that had kept her laughing for at least a half hour.

"It is. Name is Tramp."

"Cool. You going to keep him?"

"Hell, no."

"Why not?"

"He's a Dennis the Menace."

"Who's that?"

He glanced at his nephew, loving the avid curiosity in his eyes. "Never mind."

"How old is her son?" Kyle asked as they pulled to a stop along the side of the house.

"Your age, I think."

"Cool. Gonna change into my swim trunks."

And he was gone. Kyle waved to the crowd at hand and yelled, "Be right back," as he darted by.

Naomi sat up. Tramp skidded to a stop near the edge of the pool, lifted his head and made a beeline for him.

"Tramp, no."

To his complete and utter shock the dog listened, slowing down, tail wagging, canine face wreathed in a smile as he greeted him.

"Where's Janus?"

"Inside," she said with a smile. "Much to his dismay."

She wore a swimsuit.

Jax absently patted Tramp's head, pretending an interest in the dog. Of course she wore swimming gear. They were at his pool. For some reason he wished she'd worn a nun's habit. He didn't need a reminder that she was a sexy, beautiful woman. Not now. Not after he'd stood so close to her and he'd felt…

He didn't know what the hell he'd felt.

"Was that your nephew?" said a voice from the pool. Tramp followed in his wake as he moved to the edge. T.J.'s eager blue eyes stared up at him, his red hair streaming water into his face, the strands turned dark by the liquid. Jax had no idea where the boy's glasses had gone, but he could clearly see something.

"That's him."

"Where'd he go?"

"To change into his swim trunks."

The kid smiled just before he plunged under water again. Jax stood by the side, watching him transform into a shimmering mirage when he pushed off the edge, and feeling more awkward by the second.

It's your house.

Yes, but he really wanted to go back inside and work. He should do that, too, because no matter how often he told himself, he would never take it easy and slow down. He needed to stay busy. The nightmares at night were too vivid for him to ever slow down. So he worked.

"Come." Naomi patted the wooden chaise next to her. "Sit and relax."

It was just a plain black bathing suit. No fancy pattern. No tiny triangles. No body-enhancing tricks, yet it flattered her pale skin and hugged her curves in a way that convinced him all the more that he should go hide inside.

"I should work." A wet nose bumped his hand. He glanced down. Tramp stared up at him imploringly.

"Even Tramp wants you to stay."

"Tramp just wants attention."

She shook his head. "You work too much."

Her daughter sat next to her, and the little girl frowned. Jax wondered if she disapproved of her mother's boss hanging out with them. He wouldn't blame her.

"Come on," she said, patting the seat again.

Don't do it. Ignore her. Go inside and work.

But her smile was as warm and as welcoming as an innocent babe's, the blue of the pool emphasizing the lightness of her eyes, and he knew if he didn't do as she asked, he'd hurt her feelings. He didn't want to do that. He didn't want her kids to think he was a snob. He wanted to make a good impression.

Damned if he knew why.

Chapter Eight

He felt tense. Why was he tense when he sat by his damn pool?

Naomi turned toward him. He flinched as if his chaise had suddenly sprouted thorns.

"You know, you could go inside and change into your bathing suit."

The sun glistened on her pale skin and he wondered if she'd put something on to keep herself from burning. He'd never seen skin so fair. It reminded him of his mother's fine china.

"I'm okay."

Tramp turned to look at him, and Jax could swear the look on the dog's face was one of question.

"It's not a crime to actually enjoy your own pool, you know."

Yeah. That's what he'd been trying to tell himself.

On the other side of Naomi, Samantha leaned forward, catching his eye. She didn't have her mother's fair complexion and he wondered if she took after her father. His gaze fell to Naomi's hand. The gold ring still glistened.

So?

If she still carried a torch for her husband it was none of his business, except he knew that to be a lie. It was time to confess, something he always prided himself on doing—complete honesty. He liked her. She might have deplorable taste in dogs, but she was funny and charming and she sure as heck didn't look like someone who'd had two kids. He glanced at Naomi's daughter again. She must have felt his gaze because she turned, gave him the world's cheesiest smile, then went back to watching her brother.

"Cannonball!"

His nephew flew through the air, landing inches away from where T.J. swam. Tramp woofed in approval.

"Stay," he told the dog.

To his surprise, Tramp did as ordered. Inside the pool Kyle broke the surface, splashed water at T.J., then shot off. Naomi's son needed no second prompting. He was off like a sprinter.

He felt someone's gaze upon him. Samantha. He smiled. She looked away, then stood. "I'm going for a swim."

Okay, so it wasn't just the widow thing that should give him second thoughts; he needed to add two children into the mix. Complicated with a capital *C*, and not because he didn't like kids. He loved his nephew. He could just tell by the look on the daughter's face she wouldn't welcome any male attention where her mom was concerned. That wasn't the only complication. Naomi worked for him. He'd never, not once in all his years of owning a business, glanced at one of his employees. Why now?

Samantha went to the far end of the pool, dangled her legs in the water. She watched what happened in the pool in between peeking glances at her mom.

"At least take off your cowboy hat," said Naomi.

He'd forgotten he wore the damn thing. The boots on his feet should have been a reminder, but he was clearly distracted. Tramp whined. He glanced at the dog, took off his hat, waved it at the dog. "Go on."

He was off like a shot, barking at the kids in the pool. For the first time he saw Samantha smile, cowering away from Tramp when the dog spotted her sitting there and recognized her for what she was—an easy mark. A tongue bath ensued.

"Stop," she cried over the splashing in the pool, using her hands as a shield.

"Thanks for letting them swim." She said the words softly, quietly, but she punctuated them with a grateful smile. "I've got to confess, this was just what they needed. They're not used to life on a ranch. The isolation was...unexpected."

He glanced at Samantha, who tried to push Tramp away. "They'll adjust."

Naomi nodded. "Sam wants to learn how to ride." She glanced over at him. "Do you know anyone that gives lessons?"

"You should talk to Claire's sister-in-law." He glanced at his hands, wondering why he felt the need to clench them. "She gives jumping lessons."

"That's right. I forgot."

"I'm sure she'd give you a deal, too."

"I hope so, because I'm a little short on cash these days." But she didn't say the words as if she felt sorry for herself. It was just a statement of facts.

"And once she learns the basics, she's free to ride the horses here if she wants."

"Really?"

Her squeal drew the attention of the kids in the pool and he knew that he was doomed. Even Tramp had gone quiet, staring at the humans across the pool.

"Yes, really."

She was off her chair and giving him a hug before he knew what was happening, and as her long hair brushed his chin and her warm body pressed against him, he was thankful for his barricade of clothing.

"Thank you," she said emphatically. "This is just what Sam needs."

"What?" her daughter said.

Naomi turned toward her kids and said, "Mr. Stone just agreed to let you use his horses."

He felt his mouth drop open. Talk about spilling the beans. He hadn't meant right now.

"Now?" her daughter asked, her eyes brightening with interest.

"Can I ride, too?" asked T.J.

"Once you guys learn the basics," she said. "I'm going to ask Claire's sister-in-law to give you some lessons. But once you're given the all clear, you can ride."

If she'd expected whoops of delight, she must have been sorely disappointed. T.J. just said, "Cool," then kicked his way over to the side of the pool. Samantha stared between the two of them.

"Aren't you excited, Sam?"

"Mr. Stone really won't mind?"

"Not at all."

Samantha stared into his eyes, and for the first time in a long, long time, Jax began to grow uncomfortable. It was as if Naomi's daughter suspected every naughty thought he'd had about her mother.

"Sam, don't you want to say thank you?"

"Sure." Another cheesy smile. "Thanks, Mr. Stone."

"Wh—" Naomi's sigh was one of confusion. "I don't understand."

Sam stood up suddenly. "I'm going inside."

Naomi stood, taking a few steps in her direction. "Sam, wait."

But her daughter waved her away. Tramp followed in her wake. She slipped out the gate, and Tramp stopped, sat down and watched her disappear around the side of the house. Jax could tell by the slant of Naomi's shoulders that she was devastated by her reaction.

"It's actually supercool that we get to ride," T.J. said, and it looked like Naomi wanted to hug her kid right then. "I'm excited."

"And I can help you," Kyle said.

"Really?"

"My mom and I used to live in the same place you do. I used to ride all the time and play in the hills. There's a really cool lake that you can fish in and the school's awesome. How old are you?"

"Ten."

"Cool. We're the same age. You'll be in my class."

T.J.'s face lit up. "Neat." He shoved off the side of the pool, clearly aiming for Kyle. Kyle shrieked and shoved off even though there was no hope T.J. could catch him. And that was that.

Naomi sank back onto the chaise. "At least T.J.'s excited."

"Samantha will come around."

She spun to face him, red hair backlit by the sun so that it seemed to catch fire. "I don't know what her problem is. Back in Georgia horse posters covered her walls. She's always wanted to learn to ride, but since we've moved in not once has she mentioned them or wanted to see them or ask if could ride."

He didn't like it when her eyes were dulled by sadness, which only solidified his belief that he was getting in too deep.

"She's mad about the move," he said.

He watched as she stared in the direction her daughter had disappeared. "Yes, she is, and damned if I know what to do about it."

Don't hug your boss. He almost said the words out loud, but she'd probably take it wrong. She might be Sam's mom, but she clearly didn't see the possessiveness in her daughter's eyes. Jax did. What was more, he understood. Hell, he even felt guilty about the direction his thoughts had been taking.

"Where are you going?"

He hadn't even realized he'd stood up. "Work." His gaze caught on his nephew. "Do you mind keeping an eye on him for me?"

"No, of course not."

"Thanks."

"You work too much."

Because it kept his mind off things, things like a warm smile and the way she looked in that bathing suit.

"Got a lot to do before next weekend."

He didn't. Not really. She'd done all the work.

"Do you need any help?"

"No. Stay with your family. It's the weekend. Tell Kyle to come get me when he's done swimming."

He needed to escape, to figure out what was going on, why this sudden…weakness.

"You need to get some rest, too, you know."

But that was something he couldn't do around her. Impossible to relax when he kept noticing the way the sun played with her hair and how her black bathing suit made her skin look like pearls, and how much he wanted to say or do something to bring the smile back to her eyes.

"Work is good for me."

Work is what he did best. Relationships…
those were for people who didn't have a mul-
timillion-dollar corporation to manage and a
head full of crap that always seemed to get in
the way of anything meaningful.

"I DON'T LIKE it here."

Naomi counted to ten before taking a deep
breath and facing her daughter across a glass
coffee table. T.J. was off with Kyle, the two of
them having sneaked Tramp into Jax's home.
Any moment now she expected to hear the
sound of glass breaking.

"So you're okay if we only see Nona and Papa
once a year?"

Her daughter clearly didn't like that particular
line of logic. "I'll miss them, sure, but…" She
sucked in her lower lip. "I want to go back to
Georgia. It's not too late. The house isn't sold
yet."

"Look." Naomi leaned toward her troubled

daughter. "I know this was a big change. I know it's scary."

For the first time she spotted tears in her daughter's eyes. "What's wrong with going back to Georgia?"

"Nothing, but we can't go back. It's too late. We're here now."

And in California she didn't see Trevor everywhere she went. She wouldn't have to see him in the house they'd once shared, in that broken sink that he'd claimed to have fixed but still dripped incessantly. In the faces of the friends they'd once shared, their sadness and sympathy having never faded. Around town whenever she spotted a landmark they'd once visited. She'd held on to the memories long enough. Time to make some new ones.

"You hate me."

Oh no. Not the "you hate me" argument. She took another deep breath. "Sam, trust me. This is for the best." She sensed the brewing squall—

her daughter was as tempestuous as a Southern thunderstorm—so she cut her off with, "It's a done deal, Sam. Crying won't make me change my mind."

Sam bolted for her room, but not before the tears fell. Naomi rubbed her tired eyes. She had no idea why she'd thought this would be easy. Sam had always been surrounded by a posse of friends. Naomi had known she wouldn't want to leave them. Stuck out in the middle of nowhere it would be tough to make new ones, at least until school started, and then she'd have to worry about boys. T.J. was notoriously standoffish when it came to meeting new people, and yet there he was upstairs with his new best buddy terrorizing her boss with a crazy dog.

Her boss.

A man who hid his kind heart behind a gruff exterior. Who worked his butt off to the point that he'd forgotten how to have fun. Who was in need of a vacation more than anybody she'd known.

T.J. came bursting in a few minutes later. He went straight to the fridge, opening it up in search of the ever-necessary snack, all the while saying, "Kyle's staying the night at his uncle's. We're going to get up early and go fishing. Tramp's going to stay with us, too."

"In Mr. Stone's house?"

"Yup."

"And Jax was okay with that?"

"Not really." Her son emerged with a package of string cheese. "When's dinner?"

"Half hour. I just have to put it in."

"What are we having?"

"Fried chicken."

"Cool. Maybe we can feed Kyle since I doubt his uncle will do it."

"You might be surprised."

But her son was already headed down the hall. "Gonna go play with his Wii."

And that would be that. He'd found a new friend. It amazed her. It also made her want to cry. Maybe this move hadn't been such a bad idea after all.

Just then Sam cried out in frustration from the confines of her bedroom. Probably couldn't get through to one of her old friends, or the internet wasn't working right, or her tweet hadn't gone through.

Some things would never change—west coast or east—she was doomed to be deemed a horrible mother either way.

Chapter Nine

Someone smothered him.

Jax fought his way back to consciousness, arms flailing, body jerking, heart pounding. A dream. It was just a dream. He had them all the time. Terrible nightmares, except…

He pushed the weight away.

Thanks to the half light of his alarm clock he could see the culprit. Tramp.

"What the—"

A tail thumped. The dog yawned, his big canine body sprawled up against him, paws in the air.

"You are not allowed in here," he told the dog.

Tramp just rolled onto his belly, drew his legs together and curled up next to him. The dog even sighed in canine satisfaction.

"Unbelievable."

He should push him off. Remind him who was master. Exert his will so that it didn't happen again. Except he would just end up in an empty bed, alone, staring at the ceiling. It happened all the time. Sometimes he couldn't even remember what he dreamed about. He just knew it was bad, a memory from the past that'd come back to haunt him.

He got out of bed.

Tramp didn't move. Well, from what he could see he might have moved an eye, as in he opened one, determined nothing fun was about to happen and went back to sleep.

He'd lost his bed to a dog. What had the world come to?

He pulled on a T-shirt and decided to head downstairs for a cup of coffee. It was 2:00 a.m., the perfect time to conduct business overseas. By the time he finished, Kyle and T.J. would be creeping out of bed to go fishing. As he slipped inside the kitchen his eye caught movement on the back patio. He'd forgotten to arm the motion sensors, he realized, a serious breach of his security protocol that had everything to do with the woman who sat outside.

Crying.

He didn't need the light of the moon to know what was going on, although it illuminated her white-robed form. The shaking shoulders. The bent head. The way she'd wiped at her eyes. They might be silent tears, but she sobbed and it left him utterly stunned. She was the Wonder Woman of good cheer. The Elektra of charm and grace. The Peggy Carter of get-'er-done. It was like learning his house had been built upside down.

Who knew how long he would have gone on staring at her if not for Tramp. The dog tried barreling through one of the French doors. Naomi jumped. Her gaze jerked up. It landed right on him. He saw her wipe her face hurriedly, as if she worried he might see her tears. Too late for that. Then she gave a little wave. Tramp tried breaking through the door again.

"Tramp, down."

He'd say one thing for the dog, when he decided to listen, he did it well. Clearly someone had tried to train him because he sat at the door, peering over at him as if to say, "Hurry up and open it."

Except he knew if he did that he'd go straight to Naomi, probably paws first, probably knocking her over.

"Stay."

He should leave her in peace. Keep his distance. Let her cry her sorrows away.

He opened the door and slipped outside.

"Hey," she said softly, and he could hear how clogged her nose was, further evidence that she'd been bawling her eyes out. Not that there was any doubt.

"Hey," he said back.

"Fancy meeting you here."

There she was. The woman who ate sunshine for breakfast every day. Crying.

"Are you kidding?" he heard himself say. "I'm out here all the time in the middle of the night."

He wasn't. He much preferred standing and staring out the windows of his office when sleep and his hyperactive brain collided.

"Mind if I join you?"

"Sure." But there was a catch in her voice, as if she might start crying again, and if she did that he…

He didn't know what he'd do. He knew what

he *wanted* to do. But he couldn't do that. It tore at him, too. It shocked him how much it bothered him that he couldn't comfort her.

"Couldn't sleep?" he asked. It was as inane a question as a person could ask, but he couldn't think of a single other thing to say.

"Sam isn't taking the move well."

This he could deal with. Having a sister gave him an insight into the female psyche. "Give her time. She's at an age where everything is going to be drama."

"You think?"

"I know." He thought back to when Lauren was her age. They had ten years between them, which meant he could perfectly recall her teenage years. "I remember one time Lauren planned this big outing with her friends—dinner, a movie, the whole nine yards—and at the last minute, my mom decided she wanted to go out that night instead. I was home on leave at the time, but I still remember the dustup."

She nodded, wiped at her eyes. "It's just that it's so hard being the bad guy all the time. I wish Trev—"

She looked away, her red hair burnished silver by moonlight, but he didn't need to see to know she'd started to cry again. Without conscious thought his hand moved to her shoulder, and no sooner had he touched her than he thought *what are you doing?* but he couldn't seem to stop.

"I know what it's like," he said softly. "My own parents, they're not around a whole lot." The shirt she wore had been warmed by her skin. "It's not that they're bad parents, because they're not. They're just not all that involved with Kyle. They were raised in a different era. Kids were to be seen, but not heard, and so they're distant. I know Lauren hides it well, but it's been difficult for her. I didn't realize how hard until I went to visit her and I realized she was barely hanging on and I felt like a jerk. Here I was making all kinds of money and what had I done with it?" He shook his head. "I used it to make even more money. It was a game changer for me. I realized I'd done so little for anyone other than myself, just like my parents, and so I resolved to change that. Fate stepped in because Ethan called me about an idea he had for wounded warriors, and Hooves for Heroes was born."

She had stopped crying and with his own silence came the beat of his heart.

"Sometimes," he said, "doing what's right for everyone takes a huge leap of faith, but I promise you, it will work out all right in the end."

She turned to face him and he warned himself not to move. Not to stare at her lips. Not to lean in close to her.

"You're a good man, Jaxton Stone."

No, he wasn't. He was having all kinds of inappropriate thoughts about her. Wondered what she would do if he bent and brushed her lips with his own. But he couldn't. Damn it all, he just couldn't.

It was the hardest thing in the world to let her go.

"And you're a good mom," he heard himself say, forcing himself to relax and to stand. "Have faith. Trust your heart. It'll never lead you astray."

She peered up at him, blue eyes wide and pooled with tears, her hair spilling around her shoulders and he felt himself falling…falling…

"Good night."

He ran.

HAVE FAITH.

Naomi tried to remember the words as she said goodbye to her kids the following day. She would have thought Sam would be excited. Their trip to Disney World had been in the works for so long. But her daughter still held on to her grudge. T.J., however… T.J. could barely sleep last night. He was excited about flying on his own. Excited about seeing his grandparents. Excited about the trip. Sam would have nothing to do with her. When Naomi turned her kids over to the airline escort, her face heated in embarrassment when Sam took off without her.

"Bye, Mom." T.J. kissed her, having to slide his glasses back up his nose afterward. "Don't worry. I'll talk to her."

"Thanks, kiddo."

"And I'll come back with some Mickey Mouse ears to cheer you up."

She wanted to cry. Instead she hugged him, hated to release him, wondered if she should tell Jax she'd changed her mind. But, no. Sam needed time. And space. The trip would be good for her, so she reluctantly let T.J. go.

And he was off. She watched them both disappear behind a door. Their grandparents would meet them in Florida. Afterward, they'd all fly back to Georgia together. That hadn't been the original plan, but Sam had begged Naomi to let her go to Georgia with them. One last time to see her friends, she'd said, and Naomi hadn't had the heart to say no. Rose and Walt would finish packing up their house with the kids' help and then fly out to their new home in the desert with the kids in tow. They'd all be living in California then. They could settle into a routine. Well, as routine as it would get.

Because she had a crush on Jax Stone.

Her first crush since Trevor. Oh, there'd been interest from the opposite sex, but she'd turned them down cold. Nobody could ever fill the shoes of Trevor. She'd been convinced of it… until she'd met Jax. Was it any wonder, though? They were so much alike. Both gave so much of themselves. They would do anything for friends and family. They would never turn their back on someone in need. They'd both served their country. One of them had died for it. But the sad truth was she could never let her feel-

ings for him get out of hand. Sam would dis-
own her if she threw dating someone into the
whole mix.

Naomi barely recalled the drive back to the
ranch. All she could think about was how much
of a fool she was. Jax was her boss. Yet her
heart began to beat when the ranch came back
into view. She wondered if he'd meet her outside, or if she'd see him later, by the pool. If
he'd touch her again.

He was nowhere in sight and she had to fight
back disappointment. Janus was the only one to
greet her, his paws scratching at the door before
she opened it. The dog looked past her.

"They're gone." He must have picked up
the sadness in her voice because he stepped
back and then bumped his head into her hand.
"You're here, though, aren't you?" And Tramp.
Although, the dog was living with Jax, something she would have never believed possible
when she'd first met the man. They'd had no

luck finding his owner. No chip. No nothing. Jax hadn't said a word about her failure. He'd just taken the dog in—further proof that her boss was just about the nicest guy she'd ever met.

Should she go outside? To the pool? Was that too obvious? And what if she did? What if he went out there and touched her again and she felt the same thing? What if she wanted to bury herself in his arms, to inhale the scent of him, to lean back and...

No. She wouldn't go down that road. Instead she told herself to stop it. She refused to be "that woman," the one who threw herself at her boss. So she stayed up until she knew her kids had made it to Florida safe and sound, and then she went to bed, though she couldn't keep herself from peeking outside from time to time.

She tossed and turned all night. Janus crawled into bed with her at some point, nearly suffocating her until she won the battle for the pillow, but her dreams were haunted by Jax. When she woke up, she listened for him. All was quiet.

She found out why a half hour later.

She had a message from him, and her smile faded when she read it. He'd left. Work had called him away. He'd asked her to keep an eye on Tramp, which was about as close he'd come to admitting he was keeping the dog as she'd expect. He also told her the Hooves for Heroes open house was in her hands. She'd be in charge of helping to get their new ranch manager settled in, too. She read it and then reread it. The message shouldn't come as a surprise. He'd told her his job took him all over the world at the drop of a hat. That was why he'd needed a live-at-home caretaker, but with everything going on this week, it still surprised her. She would have thought he'd want to be on hand to keep an eye on things. Instead he'd given her instructions on which apartment their new ranch manager would live in, and how to get in touch with the hippotherapist, and then left without so much as a goodbye and it…stung.

Why did it sting? It was no more than she should expect. He was her boss, nothing more.

Which was why she needed to stop this right now. She couldn't get caught up in feelings for him. She doubted she would ever truly let go of Trevor. Not really. Whatever feelings she might develop for Jax, they'd be short-lived at best. That was the way these things went. Bright sparks that always fizzled.

Always.

Chapter Ten

The sun was setting when his wheels touched down at the Santa Barbara airport.

"Have a safe drive home, Mr. S," his pilot of ten years, Ben, said. The man had flown for the Navy before becoming a private pilot and Jax didn't know what he'd do without him.

"Thanks, Ben. Have a great weekend."

He'd stayed away an entire five days. Honestly, he hadn't needed to, he'd just felt it would be more prudent given the thoughts that'd gone through his head. He might have cut it a little too close, though. The big party was due to start in a few hours and he had no idea if they were ready or not. When he slipped into his truck, which he'd left parked at the airport, he realized he had less than three hours to get back to the ranch, check to ensure all was ready and get dressed. It'd been a huge leap of faith to leave everything in Naomi's hands, but somehow he knew she wouldn't disappoint.

Sure enough, when he pulled in less than an hour later, she already had signs in place directing people to park at the barn. That was where she was, he would bet, because his house was completely deserted. He debated whether or not to head down that way, but he decided to text her instead.

Home.

That was all he said. He let himself inside, pausing by his front door to listen for the clatter of dog paws on marble. She must have Tramp with her, and it was funny because he almost felt something like disappointment that the big dog wasn't around.

His phone chimed.

Welcome back! All is ready. Can't wait for you to see what we've done. You should come look.

He wanted to do exactly that. What he wanted more than that, however, was to see her again. It took every ounce of his willpower to type:

Tired. See you in a bit.

He *was* tired. A six-hour flight on Monday to New York where he'd visited clients for a day, followed by a twelve-hour flight overseas to settle the feathers of yet another big client. Twenty-four hours on the ground, followed by a flight back to New York. They'd hit a hell of a headwind on the way home. Ben had said the jet stream wreaked havoc on the arrival times of commercial airlines across the nation. It seemed to take forever to get back home and now here he was. Jet lag didn't begin to describe how he felt.

Somehow he managed to squeeze himself into a penguin suit. They were trying to impress, she'd said in one of her emails, and she didn't think cowboy boots and jeans made any kind of statement. He would wear the damn tux, but his cowboy hat would still be on his head. That he refused to give up.

Why are you avoiding her?

He should be down at the arena, making sure everything was okay. Helping out. Checking that nothing had been forgotten. Instead he was hiding out in his home like a damn fugitive and waiting until the last minute to drive down. The party would start in a half hour, their first guests could start arriving at any moment, and he figured he'd cut it as close as he could.

Behaving like a damn chicken, that's what you're doing.

The sun had long since set, and so it was in total darkness that he headed to the arena. She'd bought solar lights, he noticed, to help guide guests down the road. Smart. He was sure it was the first of many finishing touches she'd arranged for the night.

He damn near hit the brakes, though, when he spotted the arena. Just in case someone might have trouble finding the place, she'd rented spotlights. They lit up his property and drew patterns in the sky. As he drove closer he could see that the massive double doors that usually closed off the arena were now open. Inside he spotted the big-top circus tent she'd rented. The pointy part stood dead center. The doors to the barn aisle were open, too, but she'd somehow managed to light the "HFH" carved above the door.

"Can I help you?" said a man he didn't recognize and it instantly set his survival instincts atwitter. It didn't matter that he was at his own ranch, and that logic dictated the man was one of the waitstaff Naomi had hired; he instantly found himself surveying the man for a weapon.

Stop it.

His time overseas had messed with his head. This wasn't the Middle East. He was in Southern California, at a ranch he'd built to help men who suffered from PTSD way worse than he did.

"I'm looking for Naomi."

The man smiled, nodded. "She's right over there."

He pointed toward the big top. On a wooden floor there were dinner tables set up beneath the circus tent, and Naomi stood on the far side of them all, by what looked like a buffet table, talking to a woman wearing the same type of outfit as the man who'd greeted him.

"Thanks."

A horse nickered, and it was the only sign this was, in fact, an arena and a barn. The animals that would serve as center stage to his program each had their own nameplate now, and she'd had some type of rubber floor put down, presumably so their guests could wander down the aisle without fear of dirtying their shoes. Whether it was temporary or permanent, he didn't know, but he would bet it'd all cost him a pretty penny. How much, he didn't know. Frankly, he really didn't care. Traveling to a different continent had been good for him. It'd reminded him of how tough other countries had it. Visiting with his overseas staff, many of whom had been with him for years and had the battle scars to prove it, had helped him to recall his purpose back at home. Of what he wanted to accomplish, even though it hadn't lessened his thoughts about Naomi one little bit.

She turned toward him then, and her whole face lit up when she saw him, and he tripped on the floor. That's what he told himself, but deep inside he knew he lied.

Holy—

She looked like an actress on the red carpet. Or a model about to walk the runway. Or a woman born to play hostess, in her strapless red dress that hugged her upper body and then flared into a long skirt beneath.

"My liege," she said with a twinkle in her eyes.

God, he'd missed her.

How it was possible that he could know someone such a short time and already come to crave her warm smiles and irreverent humor was anybody's guess. The last time he'd seen her she'd had tears in her eyes, so he knew that at times it was all an act. That deep inside she was still haunted by the loss of her husband. That she missed Trevor and would probably go on missing him for the rest of her life. That she felt bad about uprooting her kids, even if it was for the best. One of those kids, Samantha, was all the more reason to put an end to this…this…whatever it was he felt for her. Her daughter clearly didn't want her mom to see other men.

"Nice dress," he heard himself say.

She glanced down, spread her arms as if surveying herself for the first time. "This old thing? I've had it forever." But her eyes told him she was joking. "It's actually Natalie's. She wore it to some big movie premier. Did you know she's friends with Rand Jefferson?"

All he could do was nod because he'd somehow lost the ability to talk. He had never, not in his life, seen a woman look as beautiful as she did with her hair piled high on her head and her flawless face.

"And that's my other big surprise. Guess who's coming tonight?"

He had to clear his throat. "Rand."

"Yes." She bounced up on his toes. "And he's invited all his Hollywood friends and it's going to be crazy, Jax. I've been dying to tell you, but I wanted to see your face. We're going to have paparazzi here tonight. The media exposure will be out of this world. I'm so excited for Hooves for Heroes I could just spit."

He bet she would, too. Despite looking like the cover of a magazine, he had no doubt that she was the type of woman who could hawk a loogie as well as the boys—she was just that type.

His type.

He'd spent a week away from her and rather than cool the flames, it'd only fanned them.

And all he managed to say was, "Please don't spit." Which made her smile, at least until he asked, "How are the kids?"

"Good." She forced a smile. "T.J.'s having a great time. Sam and I sort of talked it out. I think Rose and Walt had a talk with her." At his look of confusion she said, "That's their grandparents. They've asked if they can keep the kids with them in Georgia for a few more days once they get back from Disney World."

Which meant he'd have her to himself for a few more days.

Stop. You should not be thinking about her like that.

Who was he kidding?

He'd been thinking about her all week. Had she not been his employee he would have called her up, checked on her, asked how she was coping with Sam's hostility, but he hadn't wanted to cross the line.

"Come on. Let me show you what we've done." She hooked an arm through his own and it was all he could do not to pull away. She smelled like cotton candy. It baffled him how one second he wanted to put some distance between them and the next he wanted to lean into her.

"We're using half the arena because the Reynoldses are doing a special performance at the other end. I can't wait to see what they've cooked up. I have the barbecue guy out front. That's what you smell. He's got prime rib slow cooking out there. Doesn't it smell divine?"

She smelled divine.

"Amanda is in charge of the waitstaff." She drew him toward the barn aisle. "And I hired a few people to guard the front gate. They'll be checking names to make sure nobody crashes the party, but I made a deal with a few members of the media. They'll be in the background taking pictures, but I gave them strict instructions about approaching our guests. If they want an interview they have to clear it with me first." They paused in the middle of the floor. "Don't the decorations look great?"

Decorations? He hadn't even noticed. He could barely tear his eyes off her animated face.

"I love the popcorn containers. And the gerbera daisies are so bright and cheerful." For the first time the light in her eyes dimmed. "I wish my kids could see it."

"They would love it."

She nodded. "Especially T.J. He's still at an

age where everything is cool. Sam likes to think she's too old for stuff like this."

"You've done an amazing job."

She turned to face him fully, her skirt swirling around her legs. "You like it?"

"If you didn't already have the job, I would have hired you on the spot."

She smiled and he realized she had a grin like a movie starlet, the kind that could light up a screen with its brilliance.

"I can't tell you how thrilled I am with how everything turned out, especially on such short notice. I was a little worried nobody would come, but Claire started working the lines. Apparently she made a ton of contacts when she held a benefit for her son."

After helping her son battle cancer, Claire had dedicated her life to helping others. So had her son. The entire Reynolds clan was pretty amazing. He should have known they'd pitch in to help.

"It'll be great no matter who shows up."

Her expression lightened up again. "And look at you." She motioned with her hands to his outfit. "All svelte and swanky in your duds."

He glanced down at his suit. "Thanks. I think."

That expressive face of hers flickered. "You look good."

She turned away, as if she were afraid to look at him any longer. "There's Amanda. Come on. I'll introduce you."

Why did he have a feeling she was only too happy to change the subject? And why was she suddenly rushing away from him?

He hung back a second, the reason all but hitting him in the face.

Because she was attracted to him, too.

A FEW HOURS later Naomi found herself standing at the side of the arena, watching as easily a hundred guests sat or stood or milled around

Dark Horse Ranch, a feeling of pride causing her chin to lift.

"You done good, Red."

She couldn't contain her cry. "Ethan!"

Her husband's best friend opened his arms and she sank into them. She hadn't seen him since she'd arrived. According to Claire, the vet clinic where he worked kept him busy 24/7, but she was glad to see him now.

"Wow," she said after drawing back. "You clean up nice."

He glanced down at his tux self-consciously. "Do I?"

"You know you do." She glanced past him, scanning the room. "Where's Claire?"

He pointed over his shoulder with a thumb. "She's talking to one of my clients. Levi Daniels. Breeds Malinois. Lives pretty close by, but they've never met."

Claire's organization for MWDs was one of

the few approved nonmilitary rescues in the country. "I bet they have a lot in common."

She followed his gaze to the tall blond who stood taking to Claire. He had the same bearing as Ethan. Broad shoulders. Proud. "Let me guess, Marine?"

Ethan smiled. "Navy, but good guess."

She studied her friend's face, looking for signs that Ethan was thinking of him, too, of Trevor. The ghost in the room.

"You can take the man out of the military…"

"…but not the military out of the man," he finished for her with a smile.

"Do you miss it, though?" she asked.

"What? Patching together shot-up dogs? Watching as their handlers get shot, too? Dealing with…"

He didn't need to finish his sentence. He'd been her husband's best friend. He'd been the one to escort his body back home. And Janus, too. Thank goodness he'd followed the dog back to Claire's ranch and the rescue organization that'd been about to re-home him. Claire's operation. It was how they'd met.

"I better go get Claire before she goes into her 'dog breeders are bad' speech."

She smiled. "I have a feeling that man could hold his own."

"I have a feeling you're right." He bent, kissed her cheek. "It's good to see a smile on your face."

"I could say the same about you."

He smiled, nodded. "She's a remarkable woman."

"And you're a remarkable man."

He turned, but before he'd taken a step said, "Great party, by the way."

"Thanks."

She watched him cross to Claire's side, kiss her bare shoulder. He said something to her and she turned, waved. Naomi waved back.

Ethan was right. It was a good party. Everyone seemed to be having a good time. Jax could have no reason to complain about how the event had turned out. So far it'd exceeded even her own wildest expectations. The Reynolds clan had performed, Natalie wowing the crowd when she'd ridden her horse without a bridle. They'd just finished the most scrumptious dinner she'd ever had, and the best part of it all, people were hanging around for the dancing. The big band she'd hired was warming up on a flatbed trailer they'd pulled into the far end of the arena.

"Well, there's the hostess with the mostess," said a deeply masculine voice with a Texas twang.

Colby Koch.

"Howdy," she answered back.

And...*wow.*

The new ranch manager looked gorgeous in a tux he'd rented from goodness knew where and a black cowboy hat that looked the same as Jax's. A pair of eyes the same color as the big jays that perched in the trees were framed by thick, dark lashes. He might wear a hat all the time, but he was tan, and he must smile a lot because he had crow's feet, and the skin was white in the cracks where the edges crinkled.

"Quite a party."

"I know, right? I can't believe I just directed Rand Jefferson to the little boys' room."

His smile was as wide as the Texas plains he rode in from. The man was more hand-some than half the male actors who'd shown up tonight and she felt…nothing. His light blue eyes, square jaw and five-o'clock shadow hadn't stirred a single feminine bone in her body. It'd been that way all night. Men most women fan-tasized about, and they were right there in front of her, but she had eyes for only one man.

Jax.

He looked so sexy in his black tux and black hat that matched his black hair. She'd watched him smile and laugh with his guests, and take pictures with celebrities, and make small talk with starlets, and all she could think about was how perfectly at ease he seemed, and how wonderful it was that so many people had come together to make this night a success, and how she couldn't be more proud because it was clear Hooves for Heroes was poised to be an amazing success…and all because of Jax.

She had it worse than she thought.

"So have you had a chance to relax?"

"I ate dinner." Barely. She was still pretty keyed up, hoping everything would go as planned. It was all but over except the dancing.

"Then I suppose it's okay to ask you to dance?"

What? "Well, I don't know—"

"Come on." He smiled. "The music's just about to start."

As if waiting for his cue, she heard the countdown tapping of the band master, and a few seconds later the musicians started playing something she didn't instantly recognize, but by the time Colby had led her to the dance floor she had it pinned down: "Chattanooga Choo Choo." They were the only ones at first, but then she saw Natalie and Colt Reynolds head to the floor, and then Claire and Ethan McCall. They weren't much quicker than Rand Jefferson and his longtime girlfriend, who happened to share the same name as her daughter, Samantha.

"Just relax," Colby told her as they took center stage. "I'll guide you."

Guide her to do what? And then he pushed her out and she felt like a rag doll when he immediately pulled her back to him and she realized he was swinging her. Dear goodness, she hadn't done a swing dance since...

She gulped.

Trevor. They used to love it. For a moment she was overcome by sadness, but then she picked herself back up, because tonight should be a night for celebrating. And so she smiled and relaxed and Colby must have realized she knew what she was doing because he smiled, too, and soon he was pulling her out and in and around and under his arms and she was laughing. She hardly even noticed when the music changed; it was too much fun to watch her skirt swirl around her legs. Naomi would bet Natalie had never taken the dress out for a spin like she had.

"You're a good dancer," Colby yelled over the music.

"My husband taught me."

Colby's eyes went wide. "You're married."

Again the brief shot of sadness to her heart. "Not anymore." She swallowed hard. "He died in combat."

Their new ranch foreman showed he had a heart right then by squeezing her hand and shooting her a look of sympathy. "I'm sorry."

"Me, too." Okay. Change of subject needed. "Were you in the military?"

"Two tours."

She wasn't surprised. "What branch?"

"Army."

She nodded. "From Kazakhstan to cowboy. Crazy."

"I've always been a cowboy. My family owns a big ranch."

"What made you move out here?"

He shrugged, swinging her around before saying, "Needed a change."

She smiled. "Don't we all?"

The music ended and suddenly everything went quiet, but only for a moment. The soft notes of "Moonlight Serenade" began to play.

"Slow dance?"

"Sure."

"Actually," said a voice, "I'd like a turn."

Jax. If her face hadn't already been red from exertion it would have flamed brightly right then.

"You mind?" he asked her.

Yes. She minded. She didn't want to dance with him. She'd already had enough sleepless nights, thank you very much. She didn't need her imagination to have ammunition for more.

"Sure," she said.

Sam would have had a fit. But Sam wasn't here.

He nodded to Colby and she wondered if they'd met. Well, of course they had. He'd hired him—

He pulled her to him. Their hips touched and their chests brushed and it was all she could do to keep her breathing regulated. She didn't just have it bad. She had a full-on case of hero worship.

"Just relax," he said, pulling her even closer. "I'm not going to bite."

He said the last words in the shell of her ear and all she could think was how badly she wished he would bite her. She could imagine what it would be like to have his teeth lightly nip her lobes and it made her shiver. If only things were different...

"Cold?"

"No," she choked out.

I'm in lust with you.

What would he do if she said the words? Because that was what this was. She didn't believe for a moment that it was anything more. They'd just met, and he'd been so kind to her and he had such a good spirit. Nobody could build all this—she glanced up and around her—and not possess a big heart. He might try to hide it behind his gruff exterior, but it was there deep inside.

"You did an amazing job," he said, his breath stirring the hairs on her neck.

"Thank you."

"Inviting the chief of staff from the local hospital was a master stroke."

"That was your sister's idea." She wanted to lean back and look into his eyes, but she didn't dare. She was afraid of what he might see. "She thought he might be able to help refer people into your program."

"He already has." He drew back a bit and she took a deep breath before meeting his gaze. There was such a look of pride and gratitude on his face that she gulped once more. "Looks like we'll have our first guest by the end of the month."

"That's wonderful."

His smile turned crooked. She loved that tilted smile.

"*You're* wonderful," he said softly, and then he seemed a bit stricken. "I mean, you've done a wonderful job."

She couldn't look away from him. He held her hand. He drew her close and all she could do was keep on staring into his eyes, and something inside her began to swirl around, although maybe that was her head. She didn't know what this was she was feeling except it made her dizzy. Something she kept hidden within her bubbled to the surface. Her inner happiness. She hadn't had time to do anything but put one foot in front of the other since Trev died, so she'd buried her need for fun, for her kids' sake. But now, staring into Jax's eyes, she felt it gurgle to life again.

She looked away. She had to. Suddenly, she wanted to cry.

The music changed. She hardly noticed. He still held her close even though the tempo had picked up.

"Hey," he said softly. "What's the matter?"

Deep breaths. Deep breaths. Deep breaths.

"Nothing." She sniffed.

She felt him move, knew what he was about to do, and sure enough, a hand tipped up her chin.

"You're crying."

"No, I'm not," she said with a wide smile. "Just tired."

"Why are you crying?"

Quit asking me questions. "I'm not, really. It's just been so long since I danced. I'd forgotten how exhausting it is."

Lies, lies, lies. But she didn't want him to know how deeply he'd affected her.

"Do you want to stop?"

As she thought about Trevor and what he would think of her dancing in another man's arms, she instantly said, "No." Trevor would be happy for her. He wouldn't have wanted her to close herself off to the world. He would have wanted her to go on. To have fun. It was Sam who would prove to be a problem.

"Was your husband the one to teach you to swing like that?"

Could he read her thoughts so easily?

"Yes."

He smiled softly. "Well, I'm glad he did, because I'm going to make sure to dance your toes off you tonight."

"You don't have to do that."

"By the end of the night, you're going to wish you'd worn slippers."

"Jax—"

He pulled her close and she gasped, but then he pushed her out and started to slowly swing her around and she couldn't help it—she laughed. He smiled, and for a moment she was perfectly happy, but that happiness faded when she felt a tap at her shoulder. She stumbled a bit, turned.

America's favorite heartthrob stared down at her. Rand Jefferson. Hawkman. Star of big screens and little. A man voted Sexiest Man Alive last year.

And she wanted to tell him to go away.

"Natalie tells me I have to dance with you." He shot Jax an apologetic smile. "And I always do what Natalie tells me to do."

If someone had told her that she'd be asked to dance by one of America's hottest actors and that she'd actually be *disappointed*, she would have called them crazy.

"No. It's okay." She glanced at her boss.

Your boss.

She took a deep breath. "Jax should probably dance with some of his guests."

He didn't want to give her up. She could see it in his eyes and that made her want to cry for a whole other reason. He liked her. Not like a boss liked an employee. He liked her, liked her.

Dear goodness.

Heaven knew what she would do about that.

Chapter Eleven

He'd left her alone for the rest of the night. He'd had to. If he'd held her in his arms one more time he didn't think he'd let her go.

"Good night," said Amanda, the waitstaff manager.

"Night," he said, lifting a hand. "Thanks."

"My pleasure."

Was that a flirtatious grin on the woman's face? He had a feeling it was. Maybe a few weeks ago he would have taken her up on the invitation in her eyes. Right now all he wanted to do was find Naomi.

"Great party."

Colby Koch, his new ranch manager/foreman, slipped out of the shadows. "I have a feeling you'll be booked solid in a week."

"Maybe," he said, forcing himself to smile.

He hadn't liked seeing the man twirl Naomi around. Not one little bit.

"When's your fancy horse therapist arriving?"

By that he meant Brielle. "She asked for another week off. Something about a family emergency."

"Well, she better get here quick," he drawled in his Texas accent. "Gonna get crazy around here soon."

That he couldn't deny. And then he caught sight of a red dress coming from the back of the arena and he saw Colby take a step toward Naomi before he cut him off with, "Thanks for your help tonight. Naomi and I couldn't be more pleased."

He'd caught the man by surprise. Jax saw him glance in Naomi's direction, saw the question in his eyes, and he knew his new employee understood what he meant.

Back off.

"If you wouldn't mind closing up down here, I'll take Naomi back home."

He was giving the man the wrong impression. He and Naomi weren't a couple, but he was certain it sounded that way, especially when he called to her, "Ready to go?"

She was closer now, her skirt gathered in one hand, her heels dangling from her other hand, and she wouldn't look him in the eye when she said, "I can walk."

He released a snort. "You are not going to walk."

Why was she shy all of a sudden? Did Colby notice? Did he care if he did? All he cared about was that she looked exhausted and every protective instinct inside him made him want to rush to her aide.

"Come on," he said gently, holding out his hand. She stared at it, then looked him in the eyes, and he saw it then, a yearning that he recognized within himself, and every nerve ending in his body suddenly fired. Their dance. That one dance. It'd changed everything.

She took his hand.

"Good night, Colby," she said softly.

"Night," he echoed.

When they reached his truck he wanted to lift her into it. Instead he opened her door and helped her up, but his hand lingered in her own and the tension increased and he wondered how the hell he'd drive her home without slamming on the brakes and trying to kiss her.

You got it bad, buddy.

He closed her door. He almost leaned against

it. Instead he took his hat off and ran his fingers through his hair.

Get a grip.

She was tired. Exhausted. That was why she looked at him so softly. He was reading the situation wrong. He needed to rein things in before he made a huge mistake.

So he walked around the front of his truck, tossed his hat in the back seat when he opened the door, climbed inside and told himself not to look at her.

"Close your eyes. Be there in a sec."

She didn't say anything and that was good. He was grateful the drive was so short. When he pulled up in front of her apartment, he had to force himself to open the door and get out before touching her. She already had her own door open, was already slipping out, and he reached for her, to steady her, he told himself, but she reached for him, too.

"Thank you," she said softly.

"Do you need help?"

She smiled a bit. "No. Really. I'm okay."

She stepped away and his hand fell to his side and he felt such a keening sense of regret it was almost a physical ache. But then she stopped. Turned back to him, her dress once again clutched in one hand.

"Before I forget to tell you, I think it's amazing what you're doing here. You're going to help so many people. You're a good man, Jaxton Stone."

He froze. He couldn't breathe all of a sudden. She started to walk away and he rushed to her side before he could think better of it, touched her elbow, and she turned back to him and God help him, he knew he was about to do something crazy.

Just crazy.

For one terrible moment, he thought he'd misread the situation, but then the look in her eyes warmed and he found himself leaning down and kissing her and he realized all his fantasies were nothing like the reality. Every nerve ending fired. His head swam. His body heated. She tasted fifty times sweeter than anything his imagination might have cooked up, like a dessert he'd waited to eat, vanilla and chocolate with just a hint of coffee.

He pulled back. He had no idea he'd been about to do it, but somehow he did, gasping out, "We can't."

"I know."

He set her away from him. She didn't move. Why didn't she leave? Because for the love of God, his willpower only went so far.

"I loved my husband," she said softly. "He was my best friend." She tipped her head sideways, the loop of hair that'd fallen out about to completely break free. "But tonight, when you held me, Jax, when you danced with me, I was reminded of what it was like to be a woman. To be young again and carefree and it made me want…" She shook her head. "It made me want…"

He leaned forward and said softly, "What?"

She looked him square in the eye. "You."

Her words were like a sucker punch to the groin. If she knew how tightly he held onto control, she wouldn't say such a thing. She would know that he was about to do something very, very foolish. That he could only hold out for so long.

"I know this might be a mistake. Goodness knows Sam can't ever find out. But I don't care. She's not here and we are and I want…I want."

"Naomi—"

She shushed him in a hand. "I just *want*. In the morning we can talk about tomorrow. We can decide what to do about Sam, and about my future here, but for tonight… Damn it, Jax, I just want you."

He closed his eyes. How long he stood there,

he didn't know. Long enough that his knuckles started to ache from clenching his hands.

"I don't think one night will be enough."

"One night is all it can be, at least for now. At least until things settle down with my kids. I can't spring a new job and an affair with my boss on them, too."

He opened his eyes again. She held out a hand. God help him, he took it.

WHAT ARE YOU DOING? *What are you doing? What are you doing?*

The words marched the same rhythm as her steps.

It's not too late to change your mind.

She stopped in front of her door. *His* door. This was *his* place. She worked for him.

And she didn't care.

Tonight she didn't want to be boss and employee. She didn't want to think about what tomorrow would bring. She didn't want to *think*, period. She just…wanted.

She opened the door. He followed, and there came a moment when she knew she could still change her mind, when she knew she could turn to him and tell him this was a bad idea, and he would understand, he wouldn't pressure her. He would just walk away because he was that type of man. Instead she dropped her shoes and turned to him.

Janus wedged himself between them.

"Janus, no," he ordered.

"It's okay," she said. "Just kiss me."

She didn't know where the words came from, she just had a feeling if she didn't give him exact instructions he would take the chivalrous route and do something like hug her and hold her and she didn't want that. Oh no. She was miles away from her kids. Alone. In an apartment with a man she truly thought of as the sexiest man alive. Yes, sexier than Hawkman, and she was dying—no, absolutely craving his kiss.

"Naomi, I—"

She shook her head, closed the distance between them, but not before kicking her shoes into a corner and saying, "Stop talking, Jax. For the love of God, just kiss me."

And she pulled him toward her, although she didn't remember reaching for his shoulders. She knew she won when she heard him groan. She groaned, too, just before his lips found her own and she tasted the salty essence of him for the second time that night.

She wanted.

There was no other way to describe how he made her feel. He roused every feminine desire within her, even ones she didn't know she had—like the one that made her want to touch him in places that made her blush, because she'd never been the one to be brazen. Trevor had always been the instigator, the one to gently

seduce her and touch her and bring her pleasure. But with Jax she wanted things she'd never
wanted before.

She bit his lip. He gasped. She took advantage of his open mouth and slipped her tongue
inside. Even this was different. He was bolder
than Trevor, his own tongue twinning with hers,
sucking and making her groan all over again.
She arched into him, and the feel of his body
up against her own made her senses reel. She
never would have thought she'd be the type to
grab a man by the lapels of his jacket, but that
was exactly what she did. She pulled away and
tugged him toward her bedroom, although at
some point her hand slipped from his jacket
and down his arm until their fingers entwined.

What are you doing?

It was the voice of reason that asked the question. The one that reminded her that tomorrow
would come and there would be consequences
to their actions, but that had always been her

problem: she thought too much. So when she reached her room she didn't give him time to question; instead she pulled him to her again and kissed him with enough pent-up passion that he had to know she meant business.

He jerked her up against him.

Yes, like that, she tried to tell him with her mouth and her hands and her body. And just in case he missed the point, she slipped a hand between them and...

He gasped.

She pressed harder. Her zipper slipped down and it took her moment to realize he'd pulled it free. She wore no bra, so when the bodice sprang free there was nothing between them and he didn't hesitate to cup her, and she pressed against him because it was what she wanted. When his mouth broke free she mewed in disappointment, but then he bent his head and captured the tip of her breast in his mouth and she forgot her discontent because his tongue swirled around her nipple and she went limp in his arms.

It'd been so long. So very, very long...

He nipped her. She gasped, buried her fingers in his hair, shifted in a way that told him she wanted more. She knew they moved, although it was only distantly, but suddenly she was up against the bed and she didn't mind that he set her down first, or that he pulled his mouth away. She could sense his next move, and sure enough, he tugged the dress down, only to freeze when he spied her underwear. She hadn't been able to find a strapless bra that fit her right, but she'd found the sexiest pair of red underwear on God's green earth, and she'd bought them because, heaven help her, a part of her had wondered, had maybe hoped...

"You're going to be the death of me."

She lifted her hips, shoved the dress the rest of the way down. A part of her thought she should probably pick it up and do something with it because she hated to know how much the darn thing had cost; another part of her admitted she didn't care about anything other than the way Jax stared at her lying there in nothing but her scarlet-red satin. She knew she was ready for him. She could feel just how ready.

His head lowered. She started to pant. His lips found her hips first, and then his fingers brushed the wisp of fabric and she felt them move. She helped him along, wiggling out of the fabric until she lay in front of him, naked, her leg hanging off the bed, exposed to him in a way only one other man had ever seen her.

Don't think about Trevor.

He kissed her there, right there, no preamble, no gentle teasing, just his lips and the very center of her, and she cried out in pleasure as he helped her to climb higher and higher.

And then he pulled away.

Her eyes opened in disappointment. Those eyes of his. They'd gone as dark as a feral cat.

"I'm going to do things to you, Naomi."

Yes, please do.

"I'm going to make you beg me for release."

That was what she wanted.

"Turn over."

It was as if he knew he battled the ghost of Trevor. Her first love would never have demanded she do such a thing. He would have been all sweet words and kisses. Not Jax. Oh no. He urged her over, and she knew he readied himself for her. She heard the rip of the foil pouch, knew he must have carried protection with him, how convenient...

He leaned into her.

She opened for him. She felt him there and she moaned. Her hair lost its battle with bobby pins because it suddenly came tumbling down and she didn't care because he pressed into her, all warmth and hardness. His hands moved around her side to her breasts and he cupped her at the same time he kissed her and drove himself home.

"Jax," she cried.

And this was what she wanted, what she'd craved from him. She didn't care that he was her boss, and that she was a mother of two, and that her daughter would pitch a fit, or that in the morning there might be consequences. All she wanted at the moment was him inside her, and to never stop climbing higher and higher...

He gently turned her. She didn't want him to stop, but he made her slow down and suddenly things changed. Suddenly she stared into his eyes as he gently claimed her once more and her frenzied need to reach the summit subsided because there was something in his blue eyes, something that made it difficult to breathe.

He kissed her.

He still wore clothes but she didn't care because he kissed her and stroked her so very, very gently, and for some reason it made her eyes well with tears. His tongue slipped between her lips and his kiss was as gentle as the petals of a flower and pleasure began to build again, but this time in a wholly different way than before. This time her hands moved to the nape of his neck. This time she pulled him down tight, as if she could never get enough of the taste of him, and she went on kissing him and kissing him until she couldn't take it anymore and she arched and cried out her release.

He held her.

He wrapped his arms around her while she soared and glided and floated back to her.

And cried.

She cried because it'd been so long. Because she didn't think she'd ever feel the passion of a woman again. Because she'd found the perfect man to bring her back to life.

"Jax," she softly sighed.

He kissed her. She wrapped her legs around him because it was his turn. She wanted to give back. To hear him cry out in pleasure, and he must have been waiting for her because it didn't take long. Naomi felt sexier than she ever had in her life when she heard him cry out. Only then did she let him go. Only then did she pull him onto the bed with her. Only then did she snuggle up next to him and rest her head on his chest.

It was the last thing she remembered.

Chapter Twelve

He awoke to the sound of someone panting, and it wasn't Naomi.

Janus.

"Go away," he ordered the dog softly.

Janus eyed the woman in the bed, brown eyes conveying his desire to lick her face, but all it took was one softly uttered "no" to get Janus to change his mind. He scampered off to wherever he'd been hiding and Jax pulled Naomi closer. He was surprised Tramp wasn't barking to be let in, although he seemed to like the backyard.

For now all was quiet. The feel of her cuddled up next to him and the realization that for the first time in a long, long time he'd slept the whole night were revelations.

Jax glanced outside. Through a window that overlooked the back patio he could just make out the steel gray of an early dawn. Morning had arrived, and not a single nightmare had plagued his sleep.

She stirred. He held still, not daring to breathe. She lay in his arms, her hair bunched up beneath her. In sleep, her lashes fanned against her face like a line of watercolor brushes and he realized they were a perfect mirror of the shape of her eyebrows. Her cheeks were flushed, or was that makeup? He somehow doubted it, because the rosy tinge stained her jawline and hair line, and he admitted that even sound asleep, with the weakest of sunlight illuminating her face, she was still the most beautiful woman he'd ever seen.

And he shouldn't have slept with her.

His heart began to pound in a familiar way. Anxiety. A by-product of his days in the military and being shot at every day. It was why he hardly slept at night, except last night. Last night he'd slept like the dead, but now morning had come and with it cold, hard reality. Only an idiot slept with an employee. It didn't matter that he trusted her, and that he doubted she'd ever be the type to cry foul. He was her boss, and she was his employee, and she had a kid that he was pretty sure didn't like him. All of it could present some very real problems down the road.

One night, she'd said. Only he couldn't imagine never doing this again.

Quietly, gently, he disentangled himself from her arms and slipped on his pants from last night. He tossed the jacket, shirt and tie across his arm and scooped up his shoes. He told himself it was because he needed to work. He hadn't checked email in more than twelve hours. No doubt there'd be all kinds of fires to put out.

That was what he told himself.

When he softly padded down the hall to his home, he hoped like hell he hadn't woken her. He took extra care not to yank the door closed, the lock catching with a soft *snick*.

Tramp whined from the backyard. That was all he needed—a bark to wake her up.

"Shh," he softly hissed as he let Tramp inside, then he whispered, "Heel."

The dog licked his hand before falling into step alongside him. He'd be lying to himself if he didn't admit a sense of relief when he closed his office door.

"Go lie down," he told Tramp in a more normal voice.

The dog did exactly as ordered, and Jax stood there for a second in surprise. Maybe they were finally getting through to him. Or maybe Janus had worn off on him.

"You're not staying here," he told the animal. Tramp's tail thumped in response.

Work proved to be just as big a distraction as he'd hoped. He had at least a dozen messages to his home office about last night's event. People wanted to know more about the program, how they could sign up, what it cost. He should have anticipated this happening, but he hadn't and now he wondered what they would do if they ended up with more business than they could handle. So he answered emails and phone calls and he might have done so all day but for one thing: bacon.

Tramp smelled it, too; the dog lifted his head. She'd done it again. Like Aladdin rubbing the genie's lamp, she knew exactly how to summon him downstairs. Or he could open a window. It had turned into a beautiful day outside. He could hold out and go on trying to avoid her because that was exactly what he wanted to do.

His stomach growled.

"Damn," he muttered.

He stood. Tramp stood, too.

"Let's go."

The sunlight from outside painted mirror images of the window frames on the steps. The smell of bacon only increased as he stood on the landing, and still he hesitated because for some reason his nerves were stretched taut.

"Good morning," she said when he paused in the door of the kitchen, her smile as wide as triangles on a beach ball. She stood in front of the stove and something sizzled in front of her. The bacon.

"That smells good."

"Of course it does." She flipped the meat over. "There's French toast in the oven. Sit down. I'll serve some up."

"You don't have to do that."

"Yes, I do. Sit."

He watched in silence as she pulled a plate

from the oven, and then scooped some bacon out of the pan. His stomach growled again.

"Are you going to eat?"

"I already did." Her smile turned crooked, and he could have sworn she blushed because she looked away for a moment. "Worked up an appetite last night."

And she looked just as beautiful this morning as she had last night, with her hair loose around her shoulders. She wore jeans and a long-sleeved blouse over a white tank top. She'd rolled the sleeves up while she cooked, and compared to her red dress last night, the whole thing was as plain as day, and yet he found her more attractive this morning than he had when he'd first seen her across the dance floor.

"Speaking of last night," she said.

And he realized this was it. They were about to have "the conversation," the one he'd been avoiding all morning and that he'd been hoping to delay by at least a couple of hours. Leave it to her to take the bull by the horns.

"Jax. Last night was…" She worried her bottom lip and out of nowhere came the urge to kiss her. "Amazing."

He would have said mind-blowing, but he'd take amazing.

"But it can't happen again."

He froze. All morning he'd been telling himself pretty much the same thing. Yet hearing her say the same words…it took the wind out of his sails.

"My kids will be back soon. We can't ever let them know anything about what happened. My daughter would kill me, but even T.J. would probably freak out. What kind of example would I be setting for them if they knew I'd jumped into bed with my boss?"

He felt something roll around in his stomach. The bite of French toast he'd taken. It suddenly wanted to come back up.

"Add to the fact that I just moved all the way out from Georgia for this job, and so if things don't work out, I'll be out of a job, and, well…"

There was no possible way they could call this a good idea. That was what she was trying to say. What was more, he knew she was right. It was why he'd slipped from bed without her knowing. Why he'd been avoiding her. He'd arrived at the same conclusion. But knowing she was right and agreeing with her didn't mean he had to like it.

"So you want to act like nothing happened."

She nodded, and she looked so worried and sorry it jabbed at his heart. "If it will make you feel better, I'll sign something. You know. A nondisclosure agreement or something."

"Don't be ridiculous."

She was biting her lower lip again. He hated when she did that.

"You're mad."

"No," he instantly corrected. Just disappointed. She'd slipped beneath his defenses. He had no idea how she'd done it, but she had, and damned if he knew what to do about it.

"I'm not angry." He forced his tone to soften. "Hell, Naomi, I'm not even surprised. We both knew this was a mistake going into it, didn't we?"

She came around the side of the island. "Not a mistake, Jax." Her eyes were soft and so blue they reminded him of colored eggshells on Easter morning. "Never a mistake."

She would have touched him if he hadn't moved away at the last moment. He knew, though, that if she touched him, he might do something rash, something that he might regret later and that might lead to another "mistake." She knew it, too, because she let her hand fall back to her side. Her smile faded and sadness entered her eyes.

"I never thought I'd meet another man who'd

tempt me to do what we did last night." She forced a smile again, this one full of gratitude.

Gratitude.

Like he was a prized stallion and she thanked him for his service.

"You're a remarkable man, Jax."

Yeah? he wanted to say. Apparently not re-markable enough.

Chapter Thirteen

Stupid, stupid, stupid. She never should have let her crush grow into full-on lust like it had. What had she been thinking to climb into bed with her boss?

She managed to get through the rest of the day without seeing him, although that wasn't hard since it was Sunday and she had the cleanup to do after the party. She would have to face him again tomorrow, though, and she wasn't looking forward to it. At the crack of dawn on Monday, she was awoken by a call.

Georgia area code, but not her kids. Thank goodness it wasn't about her kids.

"Naomi Jones?"

"Yes?"

"This is Harrison Giles."

It took her a moment to place the name, but when she did, she shot up in bed. Her Realtor. What time was it in Georgia? She glanced at the clock and quickly did the math. It was 8:00 a.m. He'd called her first thing.

"I have some good news for you."

No. She couldn't believe it. Not this quickly.

"I've sold your house."

It was both the most bittersweet and the most beautiful thing she'd heard in years. Her house. Her beautiful house—the one she'd shared with Trevor and the kids—would no longer be hers, and though she'd been expecting the news sooner or later, she'd figured it'd be later. Way later.

"Are you there?" Harrison asked.

"Yes, of course. That's great."

"And it's for the full asking price, too," Harrison said, excitement in his words. "They absolutely fell in love with it. The buyers have family right down the street, so they can't wait to move in."

She clutched the covers up to her tighter. "That's great."

"They want to close escrow quickly. So I'm going to open up escrow at a title company near you. Where are you at exactly?"

"Via Del Caballo, California."

"Oh, wow. Yeah. I forgot about that. I must have called you early."

Her heart pounded. It was sold. So soon. "I have some stuff in the back that I didn't move out west with me. Can I have my in-laws come by and get it?"

"Of course, although I'm pretty sure the new owners would love to keep the yard the way it is."

It was her bench, the one she and Trevor would sit on whenever he'd come back from overseas. They'd planned their whole lives on that bench and suddenly she wanted it, even though she'd been telling herself for weeks it was old and falling apart and she didn't need it.

"I'll send someone over this week."

"Okay, then," Harrison said, the excitement back in his voice. "I'll send the offer over to you immediately. Do you have a fax? We'll need you to sign it and fax it back. The rest of the paperwork will have to be done through a title company."

She gave Harrison Jax's fax number, hoping he wouldn't mind her using it for personal business. Somehow she doubted he would, but it would mean seeing him again, and sooner than she would like.

"Can you send it right over?"

"Sure."

Maybe Jax wouldn't be up. Maybe she could slip upstairs without him noticing.

She got up from bed, her body still sore in places that made her blush. Best not to think about that, she told herself as she pulled on a dark green sweater and jeans. She needed to put all that behind her.

She'd sold her house.

She should be elated. It meant financial freedom. It meant she could quit her job if she needed to and maybe find another one. But she didn't want to do that. She liked working for Jax. It was a great job, and she'd always intended that money for Sam and T.J. to go to college, not for herself. It was what Trevor would have wanted her to do.

Then why did she feel like crying as she slipped into Jax's home and lightly made her way upstairs?

"You sold it."

She about jumped out of her tennis shoes. Of

course he was awake. Why wouldn't he be? The man was a workaholic.

"I sold it." She noticed a sheaf of papers on his desk, papers that she would bet belonged to her. "I hope it was okay to give my Realtor your fax number."

"Of course it is."

She nodded, looking anywhere but at him.

"You've been crying."

She jerked her head up. "No, I haven't."

"You look ready to."

Good heavens. Could he read her so well? "I'm just tired." She forced a smile. "Busy weekend."

Their night together was the elephant in the room and she waited for him to say something about it, but he didn't. Instead he slid the papers across his massive desk. "If you sign it now I'll fax it back."

"Shouldn't I read it first?"

"Of course. Have a seat."

"No thanks, I'll just bring them back—"

"Sit, Naomi. Read. And if you want, I'll read them, too."

She felt her whole body go to mush. "That's okay."

"I insist. Hand me a page when you're through with it."

She sank into his chair even though she wanted to go hide in her apartment. He was right, though. Two sets of eyes were better than one, and so she reached for the papers, although if she were honest, most of the words were a blur. Reading the offer, seeing it all there in black and white, the finality of it all.

"What's this about fixtures in the backyard?"

She looked up. "Just some stuff I thought I didn't want, but I guess now I realize I do and so I'll have to have my in-laws go and get it."

He set the paper down, his gaze intense. "This is hard on you, isn't it?"

Why did the kindness in his eyes bring her

to the brink of tears? Was it because she knew he cared for her and all she wanted to do was fall into his arms? That was crazy, because she suddenly missed Trevor more than she would have thought possible, and yet she wanted to be in another man's arms.

"I didn't expect it to sell so quickly," she admitted.

"But it's a good thing, yes?"

"It is." She took a deep breath, mostly to keep the tears at bay. "But it's also sad."

He stared at her a bit longer, but then he nodded. "It's the end of a chapter."

Despite her best efforts, her eyes welled with tears. "The start of something new."

That wouldn't include him, that couldn't include him, and that broke her heart, too. Good gracious, she was such an emotional wreck.

"It looks good to me," he said a few minutes later. "Of course, if you'd like, I can have my attorney look it over."

"No. That's okay. I'll just sign."

And she did, scribbling her name even though the letters blurred when she did. He took the document from her, stood and sent it through the printer/fax machine behind him.

"Thank you," she said.

"Do the kids know?"

Dear heavens, she hadn't even thought about that. What kind of mom was she? "No." She took a deep breath. "I think I'll wait and tell them when they get back."

He nodded. She waited.

For what?

She didn't know. She had a whole list of things to do this morning, mostly housework, so she should get going, but suddenly she didn't want to leave him.

Move.

"Thank you."

She left. He let her. She knew it was for the best. Keep busy. Keep moving. Keep ducking her head. It wasn't like she didn't have a million things on her plate. She suspected Jax would keep busy, too. She'd known the party would be a success, she just hadn't known how much until she opened her email later that morning. Messages. Dozens of them. Some from the contacts she'd made, more than a few forwarded from Jax, all of them dealing with Hooves for Heroes and how to book guests and wanting more information about the program and asking if they could take a tour of the ranch.

She didn't see Jax that whole Monday and a part of her wondered if he'd tried to avoid her. She wouldn't blame him, and, if she were honest, she was happy to have some space. She needed time to deal with the emotions that had come along with selling her house, with missing her kids, with wishing things could be different between her and Jax. Her handsome, virile boss who always treated her so kindly.

Stop.

Her cell phone rang and she about jumped out of her skin.

"Meet me out front in twenty minutes," he said without preamble. "We're headed out of town. Pack a bag."

He disconnected before she could say a word.

Pack a bag?

What did that mean? Where were they going? Was this a *date*?

Any notion that he was trying to whip her away for a romantic getaway vanished when she spotted him standing by his truck, looking the essence of a cowboy in his black hat and blue jeans. There was no welcoming smile. No nod of greeting. He'd gone back to the Jax she'd first met, the stone-faced man of few words.

"Where are we going?" she asked.

"Airport."

Wait. "What?"

He opened the passenger door of his truck, but she didn't move.

He must have seen her need to know on her face because he said, "I got a call today from a doctor back east. He saw a clip about our facility on the news."

"Oh?" She'd known the party had been picked up by the local news media, but she'd had no idea it'd gone national. How exciting. The free publicity had worked. That explained the volume of emails they'd been receiving.

"Seems he's got this guy in his care. Real bad deal. Medication isn't touching his condition. He'd been doing some reading on equine therapy and when he saw the news clip on us he said it was like a message from heaven. Picked up his phone and called me right away."

"That's incredible."

"I told him we weren't exactly open yet, but he doesn't care. Wants the guy here sooner rather than later. He pretty much begged me to take him. I figure he can help Colby around the ranch until our hippotherapist arrives. He agreed.

Told me he'd get him flown out here ASAP if I agreed, but I figured we'd go get him."

"We?"

"He's in Atlanta."

She drew back in surprise. That was only an hour or so from where she lived.

"I know. Crazy coincidence. So I figured Colby could take care of the dogs for us. We could fly back east and you could get what you need from your house, pop in and see your kids, then fly back west tonight. Maybe even with your kids if you want."

She wanted to cry. Just bawl. It was the kindest thing he could have ever offered to do, even though she knew Sam would balk at coming home early. The kindest thing *anyone* had ever done for her, really. If he was trying to knock her socks off, he'd just succeeded.

"We'll be in Atlanta by nightfall."

She hated flying, she really did, but she was so grateful all she could do was gush, "Thank you."

He nodded, swung the truck door open a little wider, his meaning clear. She climbed inside. He jumped in a few seconds later, but he didn't look at her when he started up the truck. Didn't smile. Didn't do anything other than stare straight ahead.

She hated it.

She wanted the old Jax back, the one she'd charmed out of his shell. Who'd danced with her at the party and kissed her senseless Saturday night. That was the man she'd started to fall in love with.

She jerked in her seat.

"You okay?"

She nodded, and the urge to touch him, to grab his hand, to hold onto someone solid and real nearly overwhelmed her. Not the hand of a ghost. Not Trevor's hand. His hand. And it scared the crap out of her.

"I'm fine."

But she wasn't. It wasn't just nerves about the

flight they were about to take that made her heart pound like a sledgehammer. She stared out the window at the oak trees that dotted the countryside. She hadn't pushed him away because of her kids or because he was her boss or because it was somehow wrong. She'd pushed him away because she was terrified, absolutely petrified, of loving him. There'd only been one love of her life. Just one. Nobody was lucky enough to find it twice.

Not even with a man as remarkable as Jax.

She hardly remembered the trip through the coastal mountains. Her hands had started to shake, but that was just nerves, she told herself, not anxiety about the realization that she had feelings for Jax.

"So you do this kind of thing all the time?"

She couldn't stand the silence anymore, hoped that talking would help to distract her.

"What do you mean?"

She motioned toward the front windshield,

hoping he didn't see her hand shake. "Fly out at the drop of a hat."

He nodded. "I do it when I have to. I spent a lot of years building DTS into what it is. It's my baby."

There was a tone to his voice, one that made her think he was trying to tell her something. Had he somehow guessed her feelings for him? Was he trying to warn her off? "You're lucky to be so passionate about something," she heard herself say.

He took a moment to consider her words and she told herself to relax. He wasn't trying to tell her something. But she wasn't so distracted that she couldn't admit to the truth. This was what she missed. He might seem gruff on the outside, but he was easy to talk to once he opened up.

"The men who work for me. All of them. They were handpicked by me. Their security and their safety are in my hands. That's not something I'll ever hand over to someone else."

She should have known it was something like that. His sister had told her how protective he was of her and her son.

He steered the truck off the freeway, passing in front of tall palm trees and heading toward a building with an adobe roof. Out behind it she could see jets parked on a tarmac, and beyond that, a big commercial jet starting to taxi down the main runway.

Her mouth went dry.

"Is one of those yours?" she forced out.

He pulled into a parking spot out in front of the building. "Mine is probably in a hangar for preflight."

"Do you pilot it yourself?"

She didn't know what she would do if he said yes. Probably grab a paper bag to breathe into, because for some reason the thought of him piloting a plane made her want to hyperventilate.

Instead he released a tiny huff of amusement. "Hardly. This place is an FBO. Fixed-base operator. They have hubs throughout the world." He must have seen the confusion on her face because he said, "They're sort of like jet hotels. You fly into them, you park your jet there, and if they need any maintenance, they do it for you. And they fuel them up, too."

Despite being on the edge of a nervous breakdown she heard herself say, "Because everyone needs a place to park their jet."

He smiled again. "It's a convenience." He turned his truck off.

"Hell of a convenience." She slipped out of the truck, her hair blowing back in her face. This close to the coast the wind had a kick to it. She'd worn jeans and a maroon-colored sweater, but she should have worn a jacket, too. No time to think things through.

"Mr. Stone," said a woman who stood behind a chrome-and-glass reception desk inside a lobby that looked like something out of a four-star hotel. "Your pilot said to go on through. He's ready for takeoff."

"Thanks, Kris."

The woman nodded, her grin about as sincere as a restaurant hostess's. Naomi wondered what she thought about the man in the cowboy hat and his unkempt companion with the wild red hair. She was probably used to sleek and polished celebrities.

She followed Jax through a pair of glass doors. They opened into a hangar that smelled faintly of fuel and lemon cleaner. An older man came toward them, a handsome man, one with a wide, extremely white smile and all the bells and whistles of a former naval fighter pilot, including the close-cropped gray hair.

"Mr. Stone," he said, holding out his hand. "Got you all fueled up and ready to go. Mark's already on board."

"Thanks, Ben." Her boss shook the pilot's

hand before heading toward a narrow set of steps that led up to the doorway of the jet.

If her pulse had raced back at the house, that was nothing compared to now, and it wasn't just because she'd suddenly realized she was falling in love with her boss.

"I feel like Julia Roberts in *Pretty Woman.*"

She wasn't sure Jax heard her, but the pilot did because there was a smile on his face when she glanced back at him.

"Except I doubt you're headed to the opera," Ben said.

Which meant the pilot knew his boss well. All work and no play. Why? Why was Jax so serious all the time? The only time she'd ever seen him do something fun was when he watched his nephew ride. That was it. But then she stopped inside the opening of the jet, because the posh interior took her aback.

"Wow."

Cream-colored leather seats. Plush off-white

carpet. Chrome accents. There were at least six seats, but they weren't like a commercial airliner. There were two seats that sat opposite each other with a mahogany table in between. Jax plopped down into one of those. Across from them was a couch. Beyond that were another two seats, single ones. She didn't want to sit behind Jax because to be honest, she was so nervous she didn't want to be back there all by herself. She moved because another man, the copilot Mark, she guessed, stared at her from the cockpit.

"Hey." She waved weakly, then turned to take the seat opposite Jax.

"Buckle up," Jax ordered, pulling a laptop out of a compartment in the table. "Even on a private jet you need to wear a seat belt."

"Thanks."

How could he not hear her heart pounding? She glanced out the window, at the cloudy sky. She hated flying when she couldn't see the sun.

He cocked his head at her. "You seem nervous."

Why did he have to be so observant? But she had the perfect excuse for her shaking hands. "I guess this is not the time to confess that I hate flying."

He glanced up at her casually, only to do a double take because he must have seen the terror on her face. Little did he know that the terror had a lot more to do with *him* than with flying.

"Are you okay?"

She nodded weakly.

He stood up. "Do you need something to drink?"

"Beg your pardon?"

"Whiskey? Gin? Vodka? I have it all."

Of course he did. Probably a full bar in the back of the plane. Sure enough, that's where he headed, stopping in front of a sideboard at the tail end.

"Can you bring the whole bottle?"

He grabbed something, what she couldn't see, and poured her some amber-colored liquid.

"Drink," he said, holding a crystal glass out to her.

She drank.

Whatever it was, it burned like liquid fire and it immediately warmed her chilled body. "Ugh," she said with a shutter, slamming the glass down.

The plane lurched.

"I didn't even hear him start the engine."

She had his full focus, and she didn't know if it was the alcohol or the sudden smile on his face that made her go all wonky inside. She had it bad.

"They moved it out of the hangar with a push-back."

The warmth continued to spread. She rarely, if ever, drank, and the effect of eighty proof went straight to her bloodstream.

"Oh."

Beneath his cowboy hat, his eyes watched her intently, his laptop forgotten. He leaned back.

She glanced around. "No stewardesses?"

"I don't need someone to serve me drinks."

"Maybe I should do that for you. I am your housekeeper, after all."

"You're a lot more than that."

There it was again, that intense look that made her want to squirm in her seat. She wondered if he'd ever joined the mile-high club.

Naomi.

Her flush worsened, which made her look down at her hands. Her head snapped up, though, when she heard an engine start. Any hope that flying on a private jet might make air travel feel less stressful faded when she realized they were about to depart and that she was on the verge of her usual panic attack.

"It *is* safer than driving."

"I know." She glanced out the window. "And I know my anxiety is driven by a perceived lack of control. And that, statistically speaking, only one in three million planes crash. I know that. It doesn't matter. Still scares the crap out of me."

He smiled.

No. Don't do that, she wanted to say. *Don't be kind to me. I don't need more reasons to fall in love with you.*

"Relax."

He reached for her hands. She'd placed them on the table and hadn't even known it. Or maybe she had known. Maybe deep down inside she'd wanted this, wanted him to touch her and tell her everything would be okay. Trevor had done the same thing. He'd always laughed at her irrational fear, too.

"If we crash at least it will be a quick death."

That sounded like something Trevor would say, too. "I'll remind you of that as we plummet to earth."

He laughed and she admitted she loved touching him. Maybe it was the drink. Maybe it was the feel of his hands. Maybe it was the way he wouldn't release her gaze, but calm overcame her. The jet engine revved. She realized they'd been cleared for takeoff. She knew they were moving. Slowly at first, then faster and faster, but she didn't know if it was the jet that made her heart race, or something else. Her stomach dropped as if she'd plunged off the top of a roller coaster. She held his hand tighter, and then tighter still, until sunlight suddenly blinded the cabin and she realized they were soaring above the clouds.

Only the jet wasn't the only thing soaring. As she stared into his eyes, so did her heart.

Chapter Fourteen

She'd fallen asleep somewhere over the Midwest, due, in part, to the giant glass of whiskey he'd poured her. Jax had covered her with a blanket and gone back to work, all the while marveling at how keyed up she'd been over flying. For someone so brave and clever he'd found her irrational fear somewhat amusing.

He would have let her keep on sleeping, but they'd begun their descent into Atlanta, according to Ben, and that meant he'd have to wake her soon. His pilot always insisted on seat belts, but for now he watched her sleep and he had to admit, she looked so different. She'd been really upset about selling her house. He knew why, too. She'd have to let go. It was the last of the things she'd shared with her husband. Her last anchor to her memories. That had to be scary.

He'd had a revelation, too, as they'd flown over the Midwest. He'd put away his laptop, turned off his cell phone and arrived at a decision. He wasn't going to let her slip away. To hell with the fact that she worked for him and that she had kids and that she was still hung up on Trevor. He would take a leap of faith and hope it landed him her heart because he saw in her something remarkable. A woman who'd had a tough go in life, but who'd still maintained her strength and sense of humor and dignity.

"Naomi," he said gently, shaking her lightly. "Time to wake up. We're landing."

She shot up so fast she damn near clocked him in the chin. "We're landing?"

Her left cheek was creased where it'd lain against a crack in the leather seat and her hair stuck up on one side. And yet even with her makeup smeared she still looked beautiful.

"In about fifteen minutes."

She glanced out the plane's window. It was late afternoon. The sky was a light, luminescent blue, and it meant the sun would set in a little bit.

"I hate landing," he heard her say.

He sat in his seat and contemplated what to do. She didn't want to get involved with him. Fine. He understood that, and her reasons why, but that didn't mean he had to accept them. He might be opening himself up to trouble, but he just didn't care, and so he sat down next to her, tipped his cowboy hat back and pulled her into his arms. She was stiff at first, but he refused to let her go and he eventually felt her relax.

"If we die, we'll die together," he told her.

"Thanks."

"Do you want another shot?"

She shook her head. "Only if it'll knock me out. You can wake me when we get to the ground safely."

"Come on. Let's get buckled in before Ben comes out to do his pre-landing check of the cabin. He's a bit of a hard-ass when it comes to following regulations."

She leaned away from him. "Actually, that's a good thing. It means he's conscientious and thereby less prone to crashing."

He stared at her lips, and man he'd like to kiss them, and for a moment he wondered if he should—but it was too much too soon. He'd have to woo her. Slowly. But he was patient, and in his experience good things came to those who waited.

He would wait as long as it took where Naomi was concerned.

SHE SURVIVED THE LANDING.

Jax, bless his heart, held her the whole way down. She should have pushed him away, but she hadn't. She'd succumbed to her fears and the overwhelming need to be held by him. Thank goodness he'd let her go at the end. And that he hadn't tried anything. She wasn't at all sure she'd have resisted.

"So how long will you be here for?" she asked as he drove her toward a rental car agency. He already had a car to drive—a brand-new BMW—because apparently when you had a gazillion dollars, you didn't have to worry about anything as plebian as regular rental cars. You just jumped off your jet, grabbed keys and off you went. Jax had explained there was no need for paperwork when they had a jet as collateral sitting in their hangar. She supposed he had a point.

"Just in and out. I'd like to get this guy back to

the ranch as soon as possible. Ben's on standby as I work the details out."

Another perk of being wealthy. Your own personal pilot. It was a good thing she wasn't a gold digger because it was awfully hard not to peek at the good-looking man sitting next to her and not think he was quite a catch.

"Speaking of helping someone out, I can't thank you enough for bringing me out here. I promise I'll make it quick. Shouldn't take more than a few hours to get things arranged."

The GPS shouted instructions and her stomach flipped over because soon she'd be driving home. Her last time driving home. Everything had become a list of lasts as soon as they'd landed. The last time she'd step off a plane and feel the cloying, sticky air of the South, at least until she could afford to visit for a vacation. The last time she'd ever see the inside of a luxurious jet center because she sure as certain would never be on a private jet again because she planned to fly home on her own. Probably the last time she'd ride in a car as luxurious as this one, too, although to be perfectly honest, she much preferred his truck.

"You know, I could drive you to your place."

She turned toward him so fast her rear end slid on the leather seat. "Oh no. I couldn't ask you to do that. Columbus is a million miles from here. Well, not a million, but an hour and a half. That's too far. I'm sure you have more important things to do."

He was quiet for a moment. She stared at his fingers wrapped around a leather steering wheel and tried not to fidget.

"I've got a confession to make."

The eyes beneath his cowboy hat were soft and blue and they made her want to look away. She had a feeling she knew what he was about to say. Didn't want to know if her suspicions were correct because if she was correct, that would make him the kindest, most heroic man she'd ever met—next to Trevor—and she didn't want to delve into that too deeply.

"I didn't have to fly all the way out here to pick up that soldier."

She knew it. Of course she did. If the man he'd come to pick up was still in the Army's care, that meant the Army could have made their own arrangements to get him to California.

"He's at Fort Benning, isn't he?"

"What a coincidence, right?"

Not really. It was one of the biggest Army bases in the nation. The reason why she lived in Columbus. Why she wanted to get away. Too many reminders.

"You do realize you're making it awfully hard not to hug you."

He smiled.

She loved him.

She knew it right then as he stared down at

her and admitted with tenderness in his eyes that he'd done this for her. All for her.

"Why do I have the feeling if I insist on renting a car, you'll just drive me anyway?"

"Because you'd be right."

What was with her? Why was she so emotional all of a sudden? This whole damn situation made her want to cry. It was like she was stuck in one of those horrible dreams, one where your feet were like cement bags and you couldn't move. On the one hand she wanted to turn to him and tell him she gave up. That she was willing to give it a try. To be his girl.

Her eyes began to burn.

"Hey," he said gently. "What's wrong?"

He wasn't a hard-ass. He wasn't made of stone. He was about the best man in the world she'd ever met. Who else would fly all the way across the country not just for her, but for some strange man he'd never met but whom he wanted to help.

"I'm suffering from an anxiety attack," she muttered.

He slowed down, and she knew what he was about to do.

"Jax, no."

But he pulled over anyway. They must look so strange to people passing by. The man in the luxury car wearing a cowboy hat and the woman sitting next to him with drool stains on her chin and tears in her eyes. What a hot mess she was.

"Why are you fighting this?"

"Fighting what?" she asked through a nose clogged with tears.

"Us."

Oh, dear Lord. He knew. He knew she was in love with him. Or maybe he'd just reasoned out that she'd begun to fall for him and it scared her to death. And that she wasn't the type of woman who could have sex with a man and not care.

"Jax, I—"

"Please, Naomi. Whatever there's been between us, we've always been honest with each other. You feel it, too, don't you?"

He was right. She wouldn't deny it. She was fighting this...this *thing* between them.

"I do."

Behind him, the Atlanta skyline stretched tall, a host of windows sparkling in the early-evening sunlight. This was her home. Or it used to be. A place she'd wanted to escape. To California. The land of golden opportunity.

"I don't know if I can do it, Jax."

"Do what?"

She gulped. "Say goodbye to my home."

The tears that had been hanging on by a thread suddenly broke free. She inhaled deeply to stanch the flow of even more tears, but it didn't help.

"You can. You will."

She wanted to believe him, she really did, but for the first time she wondered if her tears weren't just because she'd sold her house. If they were because she suddenly wondered if she'd done the right thing. If moving to California had been for the best. If maybe Sam was right. Maybe it'd all been a mistake, one she still had time to rectify.

Chapter Fifteen

"Mom?"

Naomi caught Sam in the midst of climbing down the stairs when she walked into her in-laws' plantation-style home.

"Surprise!" she said, suddenly wanting to cry all over again.

"Mom!" she yelled, and any fears Naomi had that Samantha might be permanently mad at her faded at the look of joy on her daughter's face. It was pure happiness. "You're here."

"I'm here," she echoed as her daughter flew into her arms.

"I knew you'd change your mind. I knew it. I knew it."

"Mom?" she heard T.J. say. His little head peeked around the corner of the kitchen and then he, too, was wrapped up in a hug.

"My word!" said a woman's voice.

"Okay, everybody, back off." Naomi looked up, meeting the gaze of her mother-in-law.

"What in heaven's name are you doing here?" asked Rose.

Naomi winced. She'd never really been close to Rose Jones. The woman and her husband loved the kids, though.

"I thought I'd surprise you." She didn't want to tell the kids that she'd sold the house they'd grown up in. Not yet. "My boss had to come out here for business and he offered to bring me along."

Sam stared up at her, disappointment filling

her eyes. Naomi stroked her head, trying to re-assure her that it would all be okay, hoping Sam wouldn't go back to hating her again when she heard the news that their house had sold. She looked into Rose's eyes, and it was clear the woman knew something was up. Naomi had never met someone who looked so stern all the time. The only time Rose's face softened was when she was dealing with her grandkids. With her short-cropped gray hair and light blue eyes, Naomi had told Trevor once she resembled her old high school math teacher, a woman who'd never liked her.

"Kids. Why don't you go upstairs to your rooms and give your mother and me some time to chat."

Sam didn't look like she wanted to leave her. Naomi often wondered if she sensed the tension between her and her grandmother.

"Go on," Naomi urged.

And still, her daughter didn't move. Naomi

shot her a silent *please* with her eyes. Sam took a step away. T.J. seemed to be waiting for his sister to set the mood because his shoulders slumped as he headed upstairs.

"Let's sit," Rose said, pointing toward the couch in the front room. Trevor had once told her that his mom loved the couch so much, she and Walt had scrimped and saved to get it, and she'd vowed never to get rid of it. Naomi was pretty sure the story was true. That would explain why Rose had never replaced it in the fifteen years she'd known the woman. And why it was harder than a park bench.

"Where's Walt?" she asked, trying to distract her.

"Golfing."

Of course he was. It was part of the reason they were moving to California. Year-round golf.

"What happened?" her mother-in-law asked the moment they'd taken a seat.

"What do you mean?"

Blue eyes just like Trevor's narrowed. "Don't play coy with me, young lady. I didn't watch you cry your eyes out for months on end not to recognize when you've been bawling."

See, and all this time she'd thought she'd done a pretty good job concealing her grief from her mother-in-law. Little did she know.

"I sold the house."

A brow popped up. She would know if her mother-in-law ever had plastic surgery because the day she could stop doing that was the day she'd had her skin stitched up. She was forever giving her the Spock brow.

"And that upset you?"

Not just that. I had an affair with my boss. And I think I'm in love with him.

It shocked her how close she was to saying exactly those words, except she didn't want to give the straitlaced Rose Jones a shock. Not at her age.

"I don't think I want to move the kids."

Rose leaned back. "I thought you wanted to stay close to us."

"I did. But then I—" *jumped into bed with my boss* "—thought about it and I'm wondering if it's really the right thing to do."

Rose crossed her arms in front of her. Naomi went on high alert. The only other time she'd ever done that was a month after Trevor had died, when Naomi had gotten a little too caught up in the grieving process, or so Rose had told her. Never mind that she'd had every right.

"You had an affair with your boss, didn't you?"

"I—" She couldn't speak for a moment. "What makes you say that?"

"The kids told me you two seemed cozy."

"No."

"Well, Sam told me that. T.J. is just like my son. More interested in fun and excitement than paying attention to what's going on around him."

I did not have an affair.

The lie was right on the tip of her tongue, but she'd never been dishonest a day in her life. She wasn't going to start by lying to her mother-in-law, and so she kept quiet. Nothing wrong with pleading the fifth—in an indirect way.

"Did he make a pass at you?"

The question almost made her laugh. Jax make a pass at her? As if that would ever happen.

"Well?"

"No."

That, at least, was the truth. She'd been the one to touch him first. Or had she been? To be honest, she couldn't remember, but what did it matter?

"So you were the instigator then." And she didn't say it like a question, she said it like a fact, and Naomi decided to take the fifth again.

Actually, what she decided to do was change the subject.

"How was your vacation with the kids?"

Rose simply stared.

"Did T.J. freak out about any of the rides?"

And still, she stared. Naomi felt her face begin to heat like a Bunsen burner. Curse her fair complexion. This was not a conversation she wanted to have with her mother-in-law. There were times when she wished she had a friend. A good friend. Someone she could confide in. Trevor had been her best friend. She'd told him everything: about the snobby mother at the kids' school. And the horrible boss she'd had when the kids were younger. Even her own suspicions that his mother didn't like her, which he'd denied, even though Naomi still thought the woman didn't think her good enough. She'd always felt like an interloper, too. Trevor had dismissed her concerns, of course, but some things never changed.

And Rose still stared.

"I think I'll go break the news to the kids."

"Sit."

She sat.

"Naomi, I'm an old woman. I do not have time for games. Something happened while you were in California. It's written all over your face. I'd like to know what."

She recognized another look on Rose's face, this one from the how-long-has-it-been-since-you've-bathed conversations they'd had after Trevor had died. Good times.

"Okay." She glanced up the stairs. The last thing she needed was for the kids to hear. "So maybe something did happen."

She expected condemnation. She expected disgust. She might have even expected contempt. But none of those emotions filled Rose's eyes. Instead what she saw could only be identified as...

Sadness.

"I've been wondering when this would happen."

As if from a distance she heard herself say, "When what would happen?"

"When you'd find someone."

I didn't "find" anyone, she wanted to say. She'd had a crush on her boss. It'd turned into something deeper. She would nip it in the bud before it could become anything more serious.

"He's just a friend."

"But you slept with him."

For an older woman she sure had a frank way of conversing about such a sensitive topic. Clearly, she'd been watching too much of *The View.*

"Just once."

And even to her own ears it sounded ridiculous. As if the frequency with which you slept with someone somehow negated the intimacy of the act. She stared down at her hands. The woman must be so disappointed with her. The glint of her wedding ring caught her eye. She played with it, wondering what Trevor would say.

"I'm surprised it was just once."

Yup. Just as she'd thought. Her mother-in-law had lost complete respect for her.

"If I'd gone as long without sex as you have, I'd have given it a week or two before calling it off."

Naomi's head snapped up. "Excuse me?"

Was that... No. That couldn't be... Kindness. Patience. Understanding. It was all there in Rose's eyes.

"Naomi, you loved my son. I had my doubts at first, I'll confess. You guys were so young. Ask Walt. I thought for sure the only reason he married you was that you must be pregnant."

It was nice to know she hadn't been far off the mark as far as Rose's feelings for her.

"But when you toughed it out all through basic training, and then you stuck with him through his first deployment, I knew it was the real deal. You loved him. What's more, he loved you."

Were those tears in the woman's eyes? She couldn't be certain. She'd never really seen Rose cry before. Not even on the day they'd buried Trevor. She'd just stood there, mute, her eyes welling with tears, but never actually crying. Today she looked ready to do exactly that.

"We were both very lucky."

"Yes," Rose said softly. "You were." She leaned forward. "But for the love of God, Red, it's time to move on."

She drew back as if the woman had hit her. Rose had never, not once since Naomi had known her, called her by Trevor's pet name.

"He would have wanted that."

"I know," Naomi said over the lump in her throat. "I hear his voice in my head all the time. He always told me if something happened to him that I was to go on living my life. That I wasn't to live like a nun."

"But that's exactly what you've been doing."

She didn't know what surprised her most: that her mother-in-law thought she'd been living like a nun, or that she heard disapproval in her voice when she talked about it.

"The next time Magic Mike comes to town, I'll invite you to come along. We can both cut loose."

But her attempt at humor was lost on Rose.

"I want to tell you something, Naomi. Something that happened a long time ago. Before Sam was born, but before I tell you, I want you to promise me that you won't be angry with me for keeping it from you for all these years."

That sounded ominous. So was the look on Rose's face. Ominous and troubled.

"I promise," she managed to choke out, even though something deep inside told her she might not want to hear it.

"It was the year Trevor was on that training mission in Germany."

No, no. She did not want to hear this, especially not now, because she perfectly recalled the time and she had a feeling she knew what Rose was about to reveal. She and Trev had been trying to have a baby, but she hadn't been able to conceive. She'd been mad at Trevor for having to take off, even though she knew there hadn't been anything he could do about it. He'd gone away in a huff, and for the first and only time in her marriage, she wondered if things were going to work out.

"He met her at a coffee shop."

"No." She stood. "I do not want to hear this."

"Sit down."

She would have done Tramp proud in that moment because she refused. "I'm serious, Rose. I don't want to know."

"You have to know," her mother-in-law said, standing, too. "For years I've watched you put my son on a pedestal, worship the ground he walked on, when all the while I carried this secret. This terrible secret…"

And it was why she'd always been so cold. It wasn't dislike. It was dismay. She'd been afraid to let something slip. Had chosen silence as a way of valor. Dear Lord. How could she have been so blind?

"He stayed there for an extra week," Naomi heard herself say.

"He was trying to decide."

Stay? Or leave.

She closed her eyes. Funny thing was, she didn't cry, didn't feel hurt, didn't feel anything because she knew. Deep inside she'd always known something had happened in Germany. She'd been afraid to probe too deep to find out what it'd been.

"So if you're waiting for this magic, perfect love to come again, Naomi, you're kidding yourself. No love is perfect. Heck. Do you know how many times I've wanted to bash Walt over the head with a golf club? That man will be buried with his nine iron."

She shouldn't find the comment funny. Now was not the time to laugh. But it was the first time she'd ever heard her mother-in-law make a funny. Even more crazy, Rose smiled, too.

"One of these days I'm going to find him in bed with his clubs, you mark my words."

Naomi smiled.

Rose's expression turned serious again. "My son was no saint, Naomi. He loved you. Of that I have no doubt. He came back to you. As far as I know, he never strayed again, and the next year you had Sam and then T.J. soon after. He was happy. Come to think of it, I don't think I've ever thanked you for that, for making my son so happy. I might have had my doubts at the beginning, but I didn't at the end. Never at the end."

How did one go from smiling to crying in the next instant? She had to wipe at her eyes.

"Thank you," she said.

Rose took a step, but she hesitated a moment before she opened her arms. Naomi took the guesswork out of the gesture. She opened her own arms and for the first time since Trevor's death, hugged Rose.

"You were good for him. You brought out the best in him."

She drew back.

"You'll be good for another man, too. And he'll be lucky to have you."

Chapter Sixteen

His house seemed ridiculously lonely without her. Even Tramp seemed to notice her absence, the animal unusually subdued.

"You miss her, too, don't you?" he asked him the morning after he'd arrived back home. She'd asked for a few days off, to think, and he'd gladly given them to her, but he hated the silence.

"To hell with this."

Tramp lifted his head again. Jax reached for his cell phone:

Took Tramp to the shelter.

He sat back on the bed. He didn't have to wait long.

What?!!

He smiled. So she wasn't completely ignoring him. Good to know.

They're prepping the gas chamber right now.

He glanced at Tramp. The dog seemed to roll his eyes. It made him smile all over again.

Haha. Very funny.

So much for scaring her.

They said they could try and adopt him out, but he's too ugly.

She replied quickly.

Beauty is in the eye of the beholder.

See, that was what he missed. Her witty comebacks. Her ability to see the humor in a situation. He missed her. The house wasn't the same without her. He missed her humming while she cleaned. He missed her dancing in the kitchen. He even missed her waffles. He didn't know what she put in those things, but he would never eat them frozen from a box again.

So he lifted his phone and shot a picture of Tramp lying on the edge of his bed, the dog doing his part by looking soulfully into the lens.

He misses you.

And Jax truly thought he did. There could be no other explanation for his melancholy. He waited for a response.

Janus probably misses you, too.

"Oh, what the heck."

I miss you.

He waited, breath held. Nothing.

"Damn it."

But then his phone beeped and his heart lifted.

I just want to say thank you, Jax. For everything.

Wait. *What?* What the hell did that mean?

He typed the words out, waiting for a response, and when he didn't get one, shot out of bed from nervous energy. Tramp didn't. The dog just lay there while he got dressed. He wondered if there was something wrong with the animal. If maybe he should call Ethan. His friend was a vet. He could maybe give him a quick once-over. Besides, calling Ethan would give him something to do. He arranged for his friend to come over and killed time by checking emails.

His inbox showed he had new messages, and somehow he knew what one of them would be. Sure enough, there it was.

"I'm so sorry."

That was the subject line. His heart started to pound as he read the content.

Dear Jax:

I know this is probably the cowardly way to do this, but I've changed my mind about working at your ranch I know, I know—after everything you've done to help me out, here I am, telling you've I've changed my mind. You must think I'm the stupidest person you've ever met.

No. Not stupid. Just very, very conflicted.

I know this will leave you in the lurch, and I'm so sorry. I guess in the end what it boils down to is I'm afraid to let myself fall again. Afraid of what it might do to me. And not just me, but the kids, too. T.J. adores you. Sam? Well, I think she suspects how I feel about you, and I know she'd come around eventually, but if I mess this up somehow, if it doesn't work out, I don't want to break their hearts again. They've already been through so much.

His gate alarm beeped—a signal that someone had arrived. A quick check of the monitor revealed Ethan driving up to the house.

I'm still planning a move to California, but we'll all live with my in-laws until I find a new job. I'll send Ethan over for my truck. Claire said they can store it until I get back to California.

I hope you know how much you mean to me, Jax. How much I admire you. You're perfect in so many ways. I'm afraid I'm not perfect enough for you.

Tramp's ears pricked forward when he heard the vehicle on the drive. His tail began to wag. He rushed to the office window, excitedly dancing around.

"It's not her, buddy."

The dog didn't believe him. Jax just sat there. He couldn't move, devastated.

The doorbell rang. Tramp barked. He thought

about ignoring him, but Ethan would just keep bugging him.

"Hey," Ethan said when Jax finally let him in.

Jax lifted a hand in greeting. "Thanks for coming over on such short notice."

Ethan cocked a head at him. "You look like you just saw your best friend get killed. What's wrong?"

He wanted to deny it. To tell his friend he was just worried about Tramp. That's what he should do.

"Naomi quit," he admitted.

Ethan drew back in surprise. "Wow." He cocked his head. "You mind me asking what happened?"

Yes, he did mind. He didn't want to talk about it. Instead he heard himself say, "Want a beer?"

Ethan called the dog over to him. Tramp reluctantly complied.

"Hey, buddy," he said to the dog. "You look okay. You missing your friends?"

"Is that what the problem is?"

Ethan straightened. "Probably, but I'll have a look at him in a minute."

Jax tried not to vomit as he headed to the kitchen. He hated to do it. It was a reminder of her. He could still see her there, leaning against the counter, a smile on her beautiful face.

She's gone.

For now, he firmly told himself. He wasn't a quitter. He wouldn't let her be one, either.

"He looks good," Ethan said, taking the beer from him. "I doubt there's anything wrong with him."

"I wish I was good."

Ethan took a swig of the beer. "Well?"

Jax took a deep breath before saying, "Your pal Trevor must have been a heck of a man."

"He was."

"She's still hung up on him. Plus, I think she's afraid of what her kids might think of me."

Ethan nodded, rested the beer on his knee.

They both looked out at the property Jax had built. At the dream they'd both shared. It was because of Ethan that he'd moved to Via Del Caballo in the first place. Because of him that he'd committed a huge part of his life, and his money, to a project that they both believed in— helping wounded vets. Ethan was a good man. If he told Jax to leave Naomi alone, he would.

"So you two hooked up then?"

Jax didn't bother to deny it.

"I kind of figured you would."

That caught his attention. "You did?"

Ethan's smile was rueful. "Well, not me. Claire predicted it. So did your sister. The two of them were like game-show hosts. Some kind of matchmaking reality flick. You should have heard them plotting what Naomi should wear to the big gala."

Jesus, Mary and Joseph. He should have known.

"Tell them thanks, but it didn't work."

Ethan glanced over at him. "You fall in love with her?"

He'd asked himself the same question a million times. "I did."

"Figured as much."

They both sat there. That was the thing about Ethan. He was quiet. Calm. Reassuring. It was what made him a good veterinarian. They'd met way back at the beginning of their military careers, had always stayed in touch, and Jax thanked God for him every day whenever he got up and looked out his front window, at the scenic valley where he now lived.

Heaven on earth.

Moving to Via Del Caballo had done more to heal the scars of war more than anything else. It'd done the same thing for Ethan. He'd have been content here. But then Naomi had come along and he realized there was more to life than his business and his home and his new ranch. So much more.

"You should go after her."

"I know," Jax said.

Ethan half turned to him, his bottle dripping with condensation. "So what's holding you back?"

Jax stared at the brown glass, observing the way the sun glinted off its surface, worked the edge of the label free while he contemplated his friend's words. "Scared, I guess. She claims she's afraid, too. I almost emailed her back and told her I felt the same way."

"She emailed you that she wasn't coming back?"

Jax nodded.

Ethan frowned. "Brutal."

Jax glanced over at him. "Thanks for your honesty."

"Sorry." Ethan stared down at his bottle, too. "You know that dog of hers, Janus? You remember me telling you about how at first Naomi didn't want him?"

Jax nodded. "Claire was supposed to adopt him out."

"She didn't want him because it hurt too much. That dog was a big reminder of what she'd lost, but here's the thing. Janus loved her. That damn dog took one look at Naomi when she came to the ranch and almost mowed her down. He remembered her. Loved her. Not the same way he loved Trevor. That was a different kind of love. That was a bond between animal and handler, a bond that was forged on the battlefield. Janus and Trevor were inseparable. When he died, a part of Janus died, too. But then he saw Naomi and it kindled a different kind of love. And then later, when he went home to the kids, yet another kind of love—protecting his young. Trevor's young. Never seen anything like it."

Jax knew what he was trying to say. He'd seen it with his own eyes. That dog loved his tiny humans. It was remarkable.

"There are all kinds of love in this world," Ethan said. "Working with animals, I've seen it in every form. Horses love their owners. Dogs adore their handlers. Hell, even cats can love."

"Surely not cats."

Ethan smiled a little, nodded. "Cats get a bum rap."

"You think."

"Pretty sure."

They both sat there in silence again. Tramp shuffled over without him realizing it, rested his head in his lap, brown eyes gazing soulfully into his own. Jax rubbed his wiry fur, leaned his head in closer.

Go get her, the dog seemed to say.

"That dog knows I'm right, too."

If only that were true. If only the dog could talk. Maybe he needed more reassurances. All he knew was that he'd never been more scared in his life. Not when he'd been in combat. Not when he'd first gone into business. Not when he'd watched his nephew fall off a steer for the first time.

"What if she says no?"

"What if you change her mind?" Ethan asked.

What if, indeed.

Chapter Seventeen

T.J. didn't take the news that Naomi wouldn't be working for Jax anymore very well. Seemed he'd had his heart set on being a cowboy, and none of the excuses she handed him amounted to any good.

"Can't I visit?" he'd asked. "I liked Jax and Kyle."

"I'm afraid not, buddy." And she hated the look of disappointment on his face. It was just what she'd been hoping to avoid.

"Plus, I'm going to look for work closer to Nona and Papa. Won't that be great?"

That had been the other surprise. In the days following their heart-to-heart Rose had really opened up. It made Naomi wish they'd spoken so honestly sooner.

"This is bunk," T.J. had said, storming off.

Sam had just watched her little brother, then fixed her gaze on her mom.

"Whatever." That'd been her response, but Naomi had seen a flash of something behind her eyes. Relief? Regret? What?

She almost didn't want to know.

So she helped Rose and Walt pack their home. Fortunately, she had the house money coming and she could use some of that for living expenses. By the time she found a new place to move to in California, the kids would be ready to start back to school. It would all work out.

"I'm going to miss this old house," Rose admitted as she slapped tape on yet another box.

"Me, too."

Her mother-in-law stared at her intently. Had she sounded sad? Was that why she looked at Naomi like that? Rose had made no bones about the fact that she thought she was crazy for giving up such a great job in California.

"It's not too late to change your mind."

"I can't do that."

He hadn't even called her. That stung. Sure, she'd been the one to quit on him, but she'd thought he'd at least put up a little fight.

"We're going to need more of these." Rose shoved the box she'd just packed off the side.

"They're out in the garage."

"I'll go get them."

"No. It's okay. I'll do it."

Trevor's mom had been working too hard. So Naomi pushed herself to her feet and headed outside.

And there he was.

He stood across the street, leaning on the driver's side of a luxury car, cowboy hat still firmly in place, and her heart leaped. It just leaped in pure joy.

He moved, opened the car door, but not before looking both ways, and she saw him then.

Tramp.

The dog had seen her, too, and it was a good thing no cars were coming because he ran straight for her, a canine woof of joy escaping just before he collided with her midsection.

"Tramp, down," she cried, blinking away tears. "You big goofball."

The dog wouldn't listen, though, just kept trying to get to her face, and she realized he wore a bow. She tried to fend him off as best she could while she watched Jax approach.

"He missed you," Jax said.

"I can see that."

"And since I miss you, too, I thought maybe we'd fly in for a visit."

Tramp finally settled down. Well, he went over to Jax next, dancing around at his feet.

"You flew all the way out here just to bring Tramp for a visit?"

He shrugged.

"I don't know what to say."

"Tell me you've missed me."

She had missed him. Terribly. He'd missed her, too. He hadn't actually told her he loved her, but she'd known it was headed in that direction for him, too. All she had to do was look into his eyes to know how right she'd been.

"Stop looking at me like that," she said softly.

"I also came to give you this." He held out an envelope she hadn't seen before.

"What is it?"

"Look."

It wasn't an invitation. It was a card.

HOOVES FOR HEROES GRAND OPENING.

She smiled. "You're finally opening for business."

"Well, we've actually been open for a couple weeks now. A soft opening. I arranged for that war veteran to come out right away. But next week we're actually cutting the ribbon. Our first guests have arrived and Colby and Brielle have both been hard at work. I'd really like you to come and see it."

"Jax, I don't have time to fly out there. I'm helping my in-laws now, and packing up the last of my own things that I need to drive out to California. There's still so much to do. We have at least another week of work…"

"That's why I'm sending my jet. You'll be back and forth in a day."

"No," she said with a firm shake of her head, trying to hand the card back to him. "I would never ask you to do that."

"I know. That's why I'm offering."

"And I'm declining."

Tramp had settled down around their feet, and he must have caught Janus's scent because he suddenly began to sniff around.

"I'm not giving up on us," he said.

"You should."

"Give me one good reason why I should."

"Because I'm in love with another man."

"You're in love with a ghost." He took a step closer to her. "With a memory."

Her heart had begun to pound in her chest. "Please don't."

"Don't what?" He took another step. "Don't remind you of what it's like to have a flesh-and-blood man? You love me, Naomi. I know you do. Maybe not the same way as you loved Trevor, but it's there."

Yes, she did, although how it'd happened so quickly she had no idea. She loved him. Terribly. Just not enough to give her the courage she'd need to take such a huge step with Jax.

"I'm sorry."

He stood there, staring down at her. "I'm sorry, too."

She bent, held out her hand to the goofy dog who'd captured her heart, too. "Goodbye, Tramp."

The dog wagged his tail and she felt tears begin to build again. She straightened, held out her hand, Trevor's ring glinting on her finger. "Goodbye, Jax."

He wouldn't take it, just turned, Tramp pausing by the edge of her yard to take one last look before bounding away.

It was the last time she would ever see him.

SHE CRIED HERSELF to sleep that night. She'd known she'd done the right thing. She was a mom. Moms made sacrifices. Right now she needed to live life for her kids.

"You told him to leave."

She'd been sitting at Rose and Walt's breakfast table, a tiny little wooden thing that would be donated to charity once they were ready to leave Georgia, and to be honest, she'd thought at first that the words had come from her own internal monologue. It took a moment to realize they'd been uttered by Sam.

"Excuse me?"

Her daughter peered at her across a plate of pancakes, her fork lifted halfway to her mouth, syrup oozing off the end. It smelled like maple in the kitchen because of it.

"Jax. I saw you talking to him, but then he left."

T.J.'s head jerked up. "Jax was here?"

His sister nodded. "And Tramp."

"Is Kyle here, too?"

"Sit down, Teej," Sam said. "It was only Jax and Tramp, and they left already."

T.J. seemed utterly devastated and it made Naomi's stomach flip.

"You had a thing with him, didn't you?"

"Sam!"

Where was this coming from? Why was her thirteen-year-old daughter suddenly talking to her like she was the adult and Naomi the kid.

"It was while we were with Nona and Papa, wasn't it?"

"What's a thing?" T.J. asked.

"Nothing," Naomi said, shooting her daughter a look that she hoped Sam knew meant she better be quiet. She should have known better.

"You've been moping around here ever since you've been back. T.J., too, although his crying I understand. He wanted to be a cowboy."

"I wanted to learn how to ride," T.J. amended.

"Same thing," Sam said before her gaze met her own. "You're in love with him, aren't you, Mom?"

"In love with who?" T.J. asked. "Tramp?"

"No, nitwit. Mr. Stone."

For the first time T.J.'s eyes lit up. "Really?"

Sam nodded, leaned back in her chair, crossed her arms in front of her. "Only Mom told him to go away." She cocked the trigger before unleashing the verbal bullet. "Because of us."

"Why?" T.J. asked. That was the thing with kids. Questions got boiled down to the bare bones.

"Because she's using us as an excuse. She doesn't want to admit her feelings to us, that she loves another man."

For the first time Naomi caught a glimpse of what this was all about. Sam was in pain. Not because her mom had fallen in love with another man, but because her own love for her father still burned brightly. Clearly, she resented her mother's ability to move on when she couldn't seem to do the same thing.

"I'm so sorry, Sam."

"For what?"

"For thinking you were over the loss of your dad."

She drew back, her eyes instantly welling with tears. "Why would you think that?"

Naomi shook her head. "I don't know. Maybe because it's been a long time since I've heard you cry yourself to sleep, too."

Sam flicked her chin up. "I'll never stop loving him, Mom. Not as long as I live."

"Me, neither," she admitted.

"But you love that man."

She took a deep breath. "I do."

"How can that be possible if you love Daddy, too?"

She shrugged. "I don't know, Sam. I just do."

T.J.'s gaze shifted to Sam, waiting for the next volley, and when his sister didn't say anything he asked, "Are you going to marry him?"

"She told him to go away," Sam answered for her.

"Why?"

"Because she thinks she needs to be some kind of supermom, I guess."

"Wait a minute," Naomi said. "I thought you didn't like him."

"He's okay." Sam shrugged, and that was probably the best she'd ever get from her daughter when it came to admitting she approved. "He's not a creep, that's for sure. And I knew it was bound to happen sooner or later."

"You mean Mom wants to be a superhero?"

Sam smirked. "Something like that, Teej."

"So you don't hate me for liking another man?" Naomi asked.

"Why would I do that?" Sam asked. "It was weird at first, seeing you flirt with him."

"I never flirted with him."

"Well, you might not think so, but I saw the way you were looking at him. It weirded me out at first, but then he flew you all the way out here just to get Dad's bench and I had to admit, that was pretty nice. But then you said you'd quit and I thought maybe I was mistaken, but I could tell by watching you I was right. You're in love with him."

She wilted back in her chair, the fight suddenly drained out of her.

"And you want to know something weird, Mom?"

T.J. stared at his sister avidly. He nodded.

"I was actually disappointed," Sam admitted.

"I'd seen you light up in a way I hadn't seen before, and suddenly that light was gone, and it made me realize how selfish I'd been."

Suddenly Naomi wanted to cry. She'd been telling herself her daughter was growing up too fast. Only now did she realize how true it was.

"You've been sad for too long. I miss you being happy.

Oh, if only it were that simple. "I'm afraid," she admitted to her kids. "No. Terrified."

"Of what?" asked T.J.

"Doing it again."

"Doing what?" This time it was Sam that asked.

"The whole relationship thing. The ups and downs. The good and the bad. The moments when you're not in love. The times you want to pack up your bags and leave. The times you're so blissfully happy you're afraid it will all disappear. The days when you're so horribly angry it's all you can do not to throw a coffee cup at someone's head. Afraid of all that. Afraid of what it means for you. Afraid of what it means for me."

There was silence around the table and she realized this was the conversation she'd needed to have, with her kids, to explain. Not keep it all bottled up inside. She'd been fooling herself. She wasn't there for them. They were there for *her*. She needed *them*. Not the other way around.

"What does it mean, Mommy?" The fight had gone out of Sam's eyes. She was her little girl again. The one who didn't understand something and needed her mother to explain.

"It means I'm in love, kiddo." She swallowed over the lump in her throat. "And sometimes love isn't pretty. It's not what they sell to you in movies and on TV. It's not perfect. It can be ugly. It can be beautiful. It can be utterly terrifying, too. It's all those things at once and

sometimes only one of those things at a time—
if that makes sense."

"It's like my Legos," T.J. said matter-of-factly.
"I would be really upset if something happened
to them. But I love my Legos. You could love
my Legos, too, Mommy, if it'll make you feel
any better."

She wanted to smile, she really did, but she
was trying too hard not to cry. "Thanks, buddy."

Sam just stared. "Did you hate Daddy sometimes?"

Naomi thought back to that time when he left
for Germany. "Yes, honey, I did, but only for
a while, and then I loved him all over again.
More, once you were born."

"And you're afraid of going through that all
over again?"

Boiled down to the nuts and bolts. "Yes. And
I'm afraid of putting you through it, too."

"So you're not miserable because of us?"

"Oh, honey." She got up from her chair, crossed to her daughter's side. "Of course not."

She thought Sam would ignore her at first. She was a teenager after all and subject to mercurial mood swings, but she felt her daughter slip her arms around her. She cuddled her head in her belly just like she used to do when she was tiny and barely stood past her knees.

"I love you, Sam."

"Don't be afraid, Mom." She felt Sam stir. When her daughter tipped her head back, there were tears in her eyes. "We'll be here for you, T.J. and me. No matter what happens, you'll always have us."

She felt her face crumple because it was true. No matter what, she would always have this. Sam in her arms. T.J., too, because he came around the side of the table and snuggled up next to her, too. Her kids. Her and Trevor's kids. A little piece of him next to her heart. Always.

"Kids. How would you like to go back to the ranch?"

T.J. jumped back. "Oh, boy. Yes!"

But it was Sam she looked to for an answer. For some reason, she needed her daughter's approval.

"I hate how sad you've become."

That was as close to an answer as she would get, but that was okay. Naomi would take it.

"Oh, kiddo. Me, too."

Chapter Eighteen

The day of his grand opening dawned beautiful and bright. Jax couldn't have ordered better weather if he'd had a direct line to God.

"It's almost a pity we're going to be inside," Claire McCall said. She paused beneath the entrance to the stable. Someone had hung a sign that said CONGRATULATIONS over the doorway and she looked up at it and smiled. "I'm surprised the horses aren't freaking out at the balloons."

Jax would bet it was Brielle who had dolled

the place up. His new hippotherapist might not live at the ranch full-time, but she made the most of her hours.

"They're therapy horses," Jax said. "Nothing fazes them."

Those horses were tied to a rail inside the arena, and Colby stood nearby. As the ranch foreman, he was in charge of preparing the animals, something Jax was grateful for. Although he'd learned a lot in recent weeks, he was no expert.

He heard someone laugh. Chance Reynolds and his wife, Carolina, stood in front of the grooming stall, Caro petting the nose of a horse. Beyond them Colt, Natalie and Lauren's future husband, Bren, stood talking to a male guest. Next to them stood another guest, a woman. Kaitlyn had been in a chopper accident. A bad one. She'd lost feeling in her right leg. Learning to ride would help her with balance and slowly build her core strength, all goals of the program.

Mission accomplished.

Jax stared down at his hands. He'd done it. He'd really done it. He'd created a state-of-the-art therapy program from scratch. He'd done the research. He'd built the facility. He'd hired the right help. Well, one of them a little too right.

Naomi.

He hadn't heard from her in the week since he'd flown to Georgia. He didn't know what he'd expected when he'd gone to see her. Maybe a pledge of undying love. Maybe not. He hadn't expected to be told that she was still in love with her husband. He understood, even suspected. It still hurt, though.

"Looks like our first member of the media has arrived," Lauren said.

Was it ridiculous that his heart rate increased when he spied not a news van, but a regular car? That he peered inside to see if it was a rental driven by Naomi? It wasn't, of course, and he felt like a fool for even considering it.

It was a pattern that repeated itself as more and more people arrived. At one point someone drove a truck toward him and he actually stopped breathing. Ridiculous. Ethan had transported her truck to her in-laws' new place in Palmdale, and as far as he knew, she was already living there. See, that was how bad it was. Every time someone arrived, his heart leaped, only to crash back around his feet. He greeted guest after guest. Jax admitted more people had shown up than had been invited. That was good. Even one of the major networks had made an appearance. He watched from a distance as they filmed Brielle working with Mitchell Robertson, a patient at the ranch.

"Uncle Jax, can I help Brielle give therapy to the soldiers? I told her I could help lead the horse around, but she said it was up to you."

In the center of the arena, Brielle walked alongside the soldier, her long blond braid swaying back and forth and she glanced from her patient to the horse, then back again. She had to help him to stay on, her blue eyes focused on her task. The man had lost the use of his legs in a recent conflict and every time Jax started feeling sorry for himself, he remembered Mitchell. Whatever life had dealt him recently, it could be worse.

"I don't see why not, as long as it's okay with Brielle."

Kyle did a jig of excitement. "She said she didn't mind as long as you didn't."

"Fine by me."

"Cool." He glanced toward Brielle, and was that hero worship on the boy's face? Did he have a crush on his pretty new hippotherapist? Jax thought he might.

"Maybe we can help that man walk again."

He forgot all about boyhood crushes then because that was the whole point. His cup should be running over. He'd built his ranch. He had guests/patients in residence. He had a full staff, and he'd inspired his nephew to volunteer his time. What more could he want?

Naomi, he instantly answered. She should have been a part of this. She was all that was missing. Her and Tramp.

He glanced around.

Tramp. The dog had been right at his feet a moment ago. He walked toward the edge of the arena, glancing around. No sign of him.

"Tramp," he called.

No answering bark. He wasn't too concerned. The dog had never wandered far. He was probably out back, in the pond. He'd never seen a dog more addicted to water, but he wasn't in the lake.

"What's wrong?" his sister asked.

"Tramp." Jax scratched his head in thought. "He's not here."

She turned in place, scouring the countryside. "Maybe he's in the back pasture with the horses?"

"He can't get in with them. Colby put that wire up last week."

His sister glanced toward the arena. "I'll go look inside."

"I'll go walk around the arena. Maybe he's off chasing a squirrel or something."

They both met up in the front of the barn a few minutes later. "Not here," his sister said, and by now Brennan had joined in.

"What's the problem?" he asked.

"He can't find Tramp."

"Did you check the house?"

Ever the efficient lawman. Leave it to Brennan to state the obvious. "I'll go do that right now."

"You need me to come with you?" Lauren asked.

"Nah. He's probably at the house like Bren says. Stay here and keep an eye on our guests."

His sister nodded. The couple laced hands as they turned back to the arena.

Jax jumped into his all-terrain vehicle. It was a short drive up to the house, and as he rounded the side of the hill, he heard the dog before he saw him.

Thank God.

He shut off the ATV and jumped out. It surprised Jax how much the dog had gotten under his skin. Last week he'd even flown Tramp up to San Francisco with him. Everyone in the office loved him. Tramp loved everyone right back, but he still missed Naomi. Every time Jax brought him home, he did the same thing. Scoured the house from end to end, always ending up at the door to the apartment. He hadn't hired anyone since Naomi had left. He doubted he would. Nobody could replace Naomi.

He heard laughter. A boy's laugh, and for a moment he thought he might have missed Kyle coming up to the house, but he'd left the boy in the arena.

"He's funny, Mom."

And he knew.

Tramp started barking again, but this time it grew louder and Jax knew he was about to be discovered, not that he'd sneaked up on them. They'd probably heard him, which meant he was about to come face-to-face with—

Tramp nearly knocked him down. "Hey. Whoa."

The dog bounced. Up, down. Up, down. And then he bounded off for Naomi, as if to say, "See who's here? See?"

I see, he silently told the dog.

"Mr. Stone," T.J. said. "It took us hours to get here. Just hours. We had to drive to my nona and papa's new house and drop Janus off. And then we had to drive here. And my mom wasn't sure if you were still having the party today so she wanted to stop off at the house first even though Sam told her nobody was here, and it turns out she was right, so we were just about to drive down to the stables, and— Is Kyle here?"

And suddenly Jax wanted to laugh. And smile. And ask him to slow down because Jax was pretty sure he hadn't caught everything T.J. was trying to tell him. By "we" he meant his mom and sister. Sam leaned against the familiar blue truck. Naomi's vehicle.

"Hey, Mr. Stone," she said, waving, looking so much like her mom in that instant even though he'd always thought T.J. was the one who mostly resembled her.

"Hey," he said back.

He looked into Naomi's eyes. Naomi's remarkable, stunning blue eyes. The ones that reminded him of secluded lakes and crystal-blue skies and precious gems all at once.

"Surprise," she said.

Boy, she had that right.

T.J. leaned up on his toes. "I'm going to run down to the stables."

"I'm going with you," Sam said, peeling off from the car. The teenager sauntered by, and

she had the strangest smile on her face. "Bye."
She gave a little wave.

And they were alone. Well, aside from Tramp.
The dog had stayed with him, eyeing his two
favorite humans as if silently asking what was
wrong with them. Why weren't they frolick-
ing through the grass and licking each other's
faces and climbing all over each other? Never
mind that that was probably the weirdest thing
Jax had ever thought of. He really had a feeling
that it was true. It made him smile. No, Naomi
made him smile.

"You're here," he said, and suddenly his smile
faded. She hadn't run up to him. Hadn't hugged
him. She hadn't kissed him. For all he knew this
was a social call and nothing more.

"I'm here," she echoed.

He didn't want to move. Wouldn't move. It
was her turn to move. He'd chased her all the
way across the country and back. Twice. Not
this time.

"Jax," she said softly. He saw her eyes change colors. They grew darker and he knew from experience that meant she was close to tears. "I just—"

To hell with it. He closed the distance between them. She opened her arms.

And he wondered if it was a dream. If he'd somehow not woken up this morning and this whole day was a figment of his imagination because she couldn't really be in his arms.

But she was.

Her heat seeped into him. Her arms held him tight. Her head tipped back and she pushed up on her toes and he bent down and kissed her.

And all was right in the world. She'd come back to him. She tilted her head sideways and he deepened the kiss and admitted he might never let her go.

A long while later she drew back. He pulled her up against him, rested his chin on her head.

"What changed your mind?"

She was quiet for a moment, and that was okay. He would have been content to hold her for the rest of the day. Hell, for the rest of his life. Until the world came to an end. She was his world.

"Sam," she said quietly. She drew back. "My daughter helped me to realize that I wasn't afraid you'd come between me and my kids, I was afraid of love itself. Afraid to surrender myself to the ups and downs and ins and outs of being in a relationship."

"And now?" he asked gently. "Are you still afraid now?"

She shook her head. "No." But then her eyes grew concerned. "But my kids. T.J. has two speeds—on and off. He's either running around or crashed on the couch. And Sam. She's a handful, Jax. She's a teen. Do you know what it's like living with a teen? And a girl teen?"

"I do," he admitted, remembering what it was like to grow up with Lauren.

"No, you don't. Or you've forgotten. It's like having Maleficent, Snow White and Elsa all rolled into one. Some days you'll want to kill her. Other days she'll make you cry, for a good reason. She'll say the sweetest thing. And then she'll make you laugh. And she'll be your best friend. And then she'll turn into Maleficent again. So I feel I should warn you, because if you're in love with me, we're a package deal. Me, my kids and my dog."

If he loved her.

"I wouldn't care if you came with a two-headed dragon, Naomi. I love you. I love everything that's a part of you, most especially your kids."

Her eyes had turned dark again, and the look on her face…it was one he committed to memory. The look of a woman who'd found the center of her universe, and never wanted to leave.

"I love you, too." She reached up on tiptoe again and he needed no second invitation. He kissed her as he'd dreamed of kissing her the past few weeks. Like a man who'd found the key to perfect happiness. And he had found that, just as long as she was always in his arms.

"Marry me," he asked a long while later. "The sooner the better. I need to make an honest woman of you in front of your kids."

She had tears in her eyes when their gazes met. "I'll marry you on one condition," she said softly.

"What's that?"

"You have to promise me that you'll never, not ever, make me mop your granite floors again."

He threw back his head and laughed, hugged her tight, kissed her again. "That," he said between kisses, "is a deal."

Epilogue

"Captain's log. Stardate 2.0.3102. Kyle and I have entered a strange new world. What appears to be a barn transformed into a church for our parents to get married in."

T.J. glanced at his cousin-to-be, a smile coming to his face when Kyle laughed.

"You really can't even tell it's an arena, can you?" Kyle said.

They were hiding out in the hayloft, a secret place they'd dubbed "the bridge" on one of their many excursions to the barn. Kyle was teaching

T.J. how to ride. In exchange, T.J. was teaching Kyle how to fish. It was something T.J.'s dad had taught him before he'd died. And that, too, was something they both had in common. They'd lost a father, but they were both gaining one on the same day.

"You think they'll smear cake in each other's face?" T.J. asked, trying to loosen the dang tie they'd forced him into. They had a perfect view of inside the arena from where they sat, hidden from everyone by a thick beam. In the middle of the arena his mom had arranged to have a temporary floor put down on the dirt. It'd been super fun to run around on it last night before they'd had to set up those darn chairs. Hundreds of them, it seemed. To his right stood an arch with all kinds of flowers and ivy and twinkling lights. It looked too girlie for him, but he had to admit, the Christmas lights around the railing and in the rafters looked pretty cool. Especially since it'd dawned a cloudy day. He and Kyle were hoping for rain.

"I'd be disappointed if they didn't."

It was Christmas Eve, although T.J. had made a face when it'd been announced that his mom would be getting married the day before Christmas. His soon-to-be aunt, Lauren, had explained to him that she'd wanted to share her wedding day with his mom. Lauren had originally picked the day because it seemed as if she and her son were getting a gift in the form of Bren Connelly. Now his mom would be getting Jax Stone and so it seemed to fit. When they'd told him that, he understood, although he'd wondered if that meant he'd get fewer presents for Christmas. He hadn't, because there was a boatload of gifts under the tree. They were celebrating tomorrow in his soon-to-be new home, a place as big as a palace, with a Christmas tree as big as the ones in the forest. Seriously. Huge.

"There sure are a lot of police officers here," T.J. observed, spotting yet another man in uniform.

"That's because Bren's the town sheriff and he knows absolutely *everybody*."

"My mom said Rand Jefferson would be here."

"I know," Kyle said, tossing a flake of alfalfa toward the ground and watching it fall to the barn aisle below.

The horses had all been moved to the pasture, which was kind of a bummer. T.J. really liked petting them.

"I've met him before, though," Kyle added. "He's really nice."

"Oh, look, here come Ethan and Claire." T.J. pointed.

Both boys watched as the couple split up outside the arena. Claire would be in the wedding. So would Ethan. The two kissed, making T.J. grimace, and then Claire headed toward one side of the arena while Ethan headed to the other. Music started to play. Some kind of fancy instrument band that T.J. wasn't really fond of, but later they had a really cool band coming, the same band that'd played at the big party his

mom had planned but that he couldn't be at because he'd been in Georgia. He couldn't wait, although it might be hot in his suit and tie. It was
supposed to get really cold later today, though,
so maybe not.

"Come on snow," Kyle murmured.

"You think it will?" T.J. asked, watching as
Chance and Carolina Reynolds also parted
company. After that it was one guest after another. T.J. lost count of how many people arrived. One of Ethan's friends, Mariah, and her
husband, Chase. Some other guy named Wes
and his wife, Jillian, and then what seemed like
half the town of Via Del Caballo.

"There's my grandparents," T.J. said, pointing to them as they took seats near the front.

"Mine are here somewhere," Kyle said, scanning the crowd for them. "First time I've seen
them in a year."

"Not mine," T.J. said. "We've been living
with—"

"Boys," someone called from down below them.

They both peered over the edge.

"There you are," said Brielle. "I've been looking everywhere for you guys. Come on."

"All right." Kyle sighed.

T.J. knew how he felt. He wasn't looking forward to walking down the aisle ahead of his mom and Kyle's mom, but he supposed it was for a good cause. His sister had to walk, too, although she was his mom's maid of honor. She'd had to dress up, too, and she didn't look half bad with her dark hair up on her head. Brielle looked better, though. Kyle said Brielle was hot. He had a feeling his friend had a crush on the older woman. He couldn't blame him, though. His mom said Brielle looked like a Disney princess, the snow queen one.

"Where have you been?" said his mom, and he stopped in his tracks when he saw her. He had never, not ever, seen his mom look so pretty in his life.

"Wow, Mom. You look great."

His mom seemed to light up. "Thanks."

"You look good, too, Mom," said Kyle.

Lauren glanced down at the dress she wore before saying, "Thanks. I think."

"You both look good," said Sam. She wore a red dress that matched the stupid ties they'd been forced to wear.

They were all gathered at the end of the barn aisle, hidden from everyone's view. They'd walk outside and around to the front, something they'd rehearsed last night, and then each of them would walk to the first row.

"We wanted to see everyone arrive," he explained.

"You guys need to get over to the other side with the men."

Kyle rolled his eyes. T.J. just shook his head. It was stupid that Jax and Bren had to stay away.

"Let's go," said Kyle.

They slipped through a door near the foot of some stairs, his mom waving goodbye, his sister sticking her tongue out at him. He just ignored her, but when he stepped outside, he stopped. Kyle did, too.

Snow.

He couldn't believe it.

"Is that really..." Kyle held out his hand.

A big, fat flake landed in his palm. They looked at each other and said at the same time, "Snow!"

They ran to tell their soon-to-be fathers. All the men—Bren, Jax, Ethan, Chance and Colt—went outside for a moment, but then they were being ushered back inside and he and Kyle had to walk down the aisle, slowly, like they'd practiced. The minister who'd be marrying his mom to Jax and his soon-to-be aunt to Bren already stood there. He smiled at him and T.J. had to admit, it was kind of cool to see all the faces staring back at him, and the arena looked really neat with all the twinkling lights and giant red ribbons tied to the backs of the chairs. The same color ribbons were wrapped around the necks of Janus and Tramp. The two leashes were being held by Brielle, and he spotted the way Kyle waved at her, although he'd probably tell him later he was just greeting the dogs, which would be an out-and-out lie, but whatever. They took their places next to the pastor, then Colt and Chance walked up and stood next to them. Ethan got to stand next to Bren and Jax.

"Here we go," he heard Ethan say.

The music got louder and Janus and Tramp started to wag their tails, the two of them having become best friends, and he realized his sister walked down the aisle. She didn't stick her tongue out at him, though. And then Carolina walked toward him in a dress that matched his sister's, followed by Natalie. Finally Claire came in and he knew this was it, the moment everyone had been waiting for.

The music changed. Everyone stood.

It was finally happening. After months of hearing his mom talk about it, and after all the problems getting things arranged in such a short amount of time, his mother would finally marry Jax, a man T.J. really, really liked. Of course, Jax would never be his dad. Well, not his *real* dad, anyway, but he made his mom happy. Happier than T.J. had ever seen her, and as he watched her say her vows he wondered if his own dad was watching and what he would think about all this. His dad would be happy for her, he decided. He'd be happy for them all.

"Ladies and gentleman," said the pastor. "I now pronounce Mr. and Mrs. Brennan Connelly and Mr. and Mrs. Jaxton Stone."

His mom turned to his new dad, and he could see that she was crying, and for some reason that made him want to cry, even though he took pains to hide the tears from Kyle. Except Kyle was crying, too, and that made him feel better.

His mom took off down the aisle toward a carriage waiting outside, the covered kind of stagecoach like you saw in the bank commercials. He hadn't even heard the darn thing pull up and it was his favorite part of the wedding. The guy said they could get rides afterward.

"You did good, twerp," his sister said, pushing him lightly while they waited for their mom and Aunt Lauren to get into the carriage with their new husbands. Behind them the wedding guests started to file out.

"You did, too," he said, glancing at the sky. Snow. He still couldn't believe it.

"I'm going to freeze walking back to the house."

The carriage took off. He caught a glimpse of his mom as she waved at them both.

"She looks happy," he said.

"She is," Sam said.

"That makes me happy."

"Me, too," Sam said.

"Here." T.J. handed her his jacket.

"You don't have to do that."

He handed it to her, anyway. He and Kyle would get warm running behind the carriage. That was the plan. And then they'd ask the guy for a ride.

"Tag, you're it," said Kyle, and then he ran after the carriage.

"See ya," T.J called to his sister, chasing after his friend.

INSIDE THE STAGECOACH, snuggled up next to her new husband, Naomi stared into the eyes of the man she loved.

"Another spectacular event planned by my wife," Jax said tenderly.

"Yeah, but this one was ever better than the last," Naomi said.

On the bench seat opposite, Lauren pulled her gaze away from her own husband and said, "It really was amazing, Naomi. It didn't even look like an arena. You should do this professionally."

She glanced up at her husband.

Her husband.

She loved the sound of that word. And as she placed a hand on his lapel, the diamond he'd bought her sparkled, and she remembered the fuss he'd made when he'd given it to her. He'd asked her to marry him again in front of her kids, but only after he'd asked for their permission. It was one of the things she loved about Jax, the way he included her kids in everything. There were other things to love, too. He spoiled her rotten. Encouraged her to explore her talent as an event planner. He even put up with Sam and her pubescent teenager mood swings.

"I love you," she said softly.

He stared down at her and she could see an answering love in his eyes.

"Just remember who said it first."

He kissed her. Across from them, Bren kissed Lauren, right as the stagecoach hit a hole that made them bump noses, which made them all laugh as outside the snow began to fall harder.

"It's perfect," she heard herself say.

Jax grabbed her hand, and she squeezed his back. "You're perfect."

This time when they kissed there were no potholes to disturb it. In the distance the kids laughed. Inside Naomi closed her eyes and kissed the man of her dreams, the man who would carry her through the good and the bad, who would shelter her from the storm and run naked with her through the snow, who would laugh and cry with her, and who would never leave her side.

* * * * *

MILLS & BOON®
Hardback – October 2017

ROMANCE

Claimed for the Leonelli Legacy	Lynne Graham
The Italian's Pregnant Prisoner	Maisey Yates
Buying His Bride of Convenience	Michelle Smart
The Tycoon's Marriage Deal	Melanie Milburne
Undone by the Billionaire Duke	Caitlin Crews
His Majesty's Temporary Bride	Annie West
Bound by the Millionaire's Ring	Dani Collins
The Virgin's Shock Baby	Heidi Rice
Whisked Away by Her Sicilian Boss	Rebecca Winters
The Sheikh's Pregnant Bride	Jessica Gilmore
A Proposal from the Italian Count	Lucy Gordon
Claiming His Secret Royal Heir	Nina Milne
Sleigh Ride with the Single Dad	Alison Roberts
A Firefighter in Her Stocking	Janice Lynn
A Christmas Miracle	Amy Andrews
Reunited with Her Surgeon Prince	Marion Lennox
Falling for Her Fake Fiancé	Sue MacKay
The Family She's Longed For	Lucy Clark
Billionaire Boss, Holiday Baby	Janice Maynard
Billionaire's Baby Bind	Katherine Garbera